DEAD MEN SCARE ME STUPID

JOHN SWARTZWELDER

Kennydale Books
Chatsworth, California

Copyright © 2008
by John Swartzwelder

Published by:
Kennydale Books
P.O. Box 3925
Chatsworth, California 91313-3925

All Rights Reserved. No part of this book may be reproduced or transmitted in any form or by any means, electronic or mechanical, including photocopying, recording or by any information storage and retrieval system, without written permission from the author, except for the inclusion of brief quotations in a review.

First Printing April, 2008

ISBN 13 (paperback edition) 978-0-9755799-8-5
ISBN 13 (hardback edition) 978-0-9755799-9-2
ISBN 10 (paperback edition) 0-9755799-8-3
ISBN 10 (hardback edition) 0-9755799-9-1

Library of Congress Control Number: 2008901007

This book is a work of fiction. Names, characters, places and incidents either are the product of the author's imagination or are used fictitiously, and any resemblance to actual persons, living or dead, events, or locales is entirely coincidental.

Printed in the United States of America

CHAPTER ONE

Well, they found Amelia Earhart. That's the good news. Unfortunately, they found her in the trunk of my car. Boy, was my face red. I had a lot of explaining to do there. And after I had explained everything, they didn't believe me! You probably won't believe me either, come to think of it. Sometimes I wonder why I bother.

It all began a few months ago. I was in the middle of a murder investigation.

"SOMEONE IN THIS STADIUM IS THE KILLER...Killer...killer," I announced over the PA system.

A mighty roar of surprise and anger went up. Everyone thought they were here for a free ball game. But there would be no double header today. Babe Ruth Jr. wasn't here, despite what the posters promised. And they wouldn't be seeing a race around the bases between a man and a tidal wave. Nor would the National Anthem be sung by an owl. It was all a ruse to get them into the ballpark so I could ask them a few questions

1

about a little murder I was working on. I'd gotten the idea for this ruse from a detective novel.

I've always been an avid reader of detective novels. They're full of useful tips that can help a detective like me—I mean one of my quality—do his job. I've always needed all the help I can get doing my job, because finding criminals is hard. They don't want to be found, for one thing. They keep moving around. It gets confusing. You keep forgetting who you searched already, and who still needs to be searched. Sometimes I wish everybody would just stand still for a minute so I could get us sorted out.

And criminals don't always return to the scene of the crime. People say they do, but they don't. So there's no point in standing there with handcuffs and a jury. Chances are, they're not coming.

If you could spot them by their criminal shape, if they were all bent and twisty or something, that would make things easier. Or if we just had to look for the blinking lights on their heads. Or their tell-tale names ("This looks like the work of I. M. Guilty, and his oriental sidekick Mee Too"). But maybe that would make the detective business too easy. I dunno. There should be someplace in the middle we could all live with. Some middle ground. The way it stands now, it's too hard.

Anyway, this ruse I'd come across in my reading involved gathering all of the suspects together in one room under some phony pretext—a dinner party or a hootenanny or something—and then suddenly bolting the door. Voila! You've got your criminal. He's in there somewhere. Now all you have to do is discover which one he is. You do this by carefully recounting all the facts of the case, event by event, clue by clue, until someone cracks and confesses to the crime. Then you turn to the cops and say "Take him away, boys!" or "He's all yours, Inspector Lazy!"—some wisecrack like that—and the job is done.

That sounded like a better plan than the way I was currently doing it, which was sitting in my office staring at the phone, waiting for the murderer to turn himself in to the police and call me up to tell me the results of his trial. Detectives get calls like that sometimes, but you can't count on them.

Assembling all the suspects in one place turned out to be harder than I thought it would be. I was going to rent a banquet room at the hotel, but after I had added up all the people I suspected, I had to rent a multi-purpose sports stadium. The biggest one in the world. The overflow I packed into the parking lot, and the rest I put in a nearby train station. One small suspect had to sit in my lap. When I was sure everyone was there, I started my investigation over the stadium's PA system.

"You people in the blimp, can you hear me all right up there?"

They signaled that they could hear me.

"All right then. Let's get started. And when you confess, wave your arms so a uniformed policeman can locate you. Now... let's see here... Seat 42A, Upper Right Field Grandstand, where were you on the night of May 16th?... Seat 42A, Upper Right Field Grandstand? Is he here?... I didn't know we had a concession stand... well, when he gets back, tell him he's got some questions to answer. All right then, let's move on to Seat 106 Left Field Loge Level. Do you recognize this topcoat? You should, because... Seat 106?... Is everyone sitting in their assigned seats? You teenage suspects quit moving around like that."

Once I had gotten everyone back in their seats, I started going over the case point by point, just like it said to do in the detective novels, putting suspect after suspect on the hot seat, grilling them as unmercifully as a person over a PA system can.

It went pretty well, though I ran into a few snags. For one thing, the crowd didn't have PA systems like mine so I had a hard time hearing their answers. I had to keep saying "What?" and "Confess louder" all the time. I wasn't sure whether they were cracking over there or not. Then my investigation had to be halted for several minutes, because of a dog being on the field.

But the biggest problem I had was that I didn't know what I was talking about. My reconstruction of the case was all mixed up, and had to be corrected by the crowd at numerous key points. The crime had occurred at night, not during the day. And the victims died after they were shot, not before. And nothing in the case had anything to do with the circus. The crowd got pretty exasperated with me there a few times. And I didn't blame them. You've got to have your facts straight in a complicated case like this. That's what I learned that day.

Once my lack of preparation had become apparent to everyone, the crowd lost interest in what I was saying and beach balls started being batted around. I batted a few of them myself. It was kind of fun, but it wasn't getting us anywhere. It wasn't what we had come for.

Finally, as it became obvious that I wasn't going to be able to nail the guilty party until I had gotten the facts straighter in my head, the crowd began to thin out as suspects left early to beat the traffic. At that point I decided I might as well leave early too.

"That was a bust," said one of the suspects as we walked up the tunnel towards the street.

"You said it, brother," I agreed. $14,082 for the stadium rental. $2500 to use the electronic scoreboard. $25 to rent the dog. All wasted.

On my drive home, I tried to figure out what to do next. Should I try the same ruse again later when I was better prepared, or just take the detective novel back to the library and throw it in the librarian's face? Option A was more likely to result in an arrest, but Option B was cheaper and easier, and more my style, so I was leaning towards that one.

While I was pondering this, I suddenly thought I saw one of my old clients under a street light waving at me. I looked in my rear view mirror, but he was gone. I rubbed my eyes and looked again. Still nothing. I shook my head to clear it. I was seeing things.

It had certainly looked like one of my old clients—a guy named Brannigan—but I knew it couldn't be him, because he was dead due to my incompetence. Like a lot of people, my blunders have resulted in the deaths of many of those around me. The man I thought I had seen had perished months ago, during what I call "The Case of the Dead Client". Actually a lot of my cases are named that. Maybe I should number them instead of naming them. Less confusing that way. But of all the mistakes I had ever made that resulted in people getting killed, none had ever come back to haunt me. Until now, apparently.

A half mile farther down the road, the same man was under another street light. He tipped his hat to me. A block later I saw him again. This time he tipped his head.

CHAPTER TWO

Now I'm not one of those guys who gets afraid of things all the time. No money in it, is one reason. No one pays you for it. No matter how frightened you get. And I'm usually too tired anyway. Being afraid takes energy. You have to run around yelling and pointing at the thing you're afraid of, and climbing over things trying to get away from whatever it is, and looking back over those same things to see if it's still coming, and so on. It's a lot of work. And, like I said, at the end of the day there's no paycheck waiting for you. So I figure the hell with it.

But ghosts are different. Ghosts scare me stupid. I don't worry about the financial end, or how tired I am, or anything else when I see a ghost. I just run. Something about being dead but still being able to scream in my face bothers me. It doesn't seem right. I mean, I'm no doctor, but I don't think dead people should be able to do that.

Because of this fear of mine, I was pretty jittery by the time I got home. I looked the whole house over carefully before I finally started to relax. All clear. No ghosts anywhere. I guess I forgot to check the bathroom though, because that's where he was.

I saw him in my bathroom mirror when I was getting ready for bed. "Hi, Burly," he said cheerfully. I let out a yell, then quickly yanked opened the medicine cabinet door and looked inside. As I did this I heard something fall out of the mirror and land in the bathtub. I turned and saw a glimpse of it as it was fading away rubbing its head. It was that same ghost all right.

I had a hard time sleeping that night. Somebody in my bedroom had the hiccups. I didn't bother to turn on the light. I knew who it was.

The next morning I squeezed him out onto my toothbrush.

"Hi, Burly!"

Horrified, I stared at him, then, still in a daze, began brushing my teeth. I hardly heard his muffled complaints.

After I took my shower, I found I was toweling off with a bigger towel than usual. And it was wearing a hat. It let out an unearthly laugh. I dropped the towel. Women screamed.

"You women get out of my house!" I yelled. They ran out, screaming. I guess I must have left my front door open. That's the only explanation I can think of.

All the way to my office I kept seeing that same ghost everywhere; his face was in every traffic light, either happy, sad, or worried, depending on the light's color; he was on every billboard, pointing out quality products he apparently felt were bargains; and for the whole drive I couldn't get anything on my car radio, on any station, except "Hi, Burly".

I tried to get some work done when I got to the office, but it was impossible. I couldn't concentrate. I kept suddenly turning around and looking behind me, because I thought I heard a ghost back there. Then I'd have to turn around the other way, for the same reason. And so on, all day long. It's hard to concentrate when you're spinning around like that.

All this supernatural stuff was really starting to get to me. I figured I must be cracking up. At first I thought maybe I had just been working too hard, but everybody I knew laughed at that idea. After awhile I laughed too. Working too hard! Me! Hah! That's rich.

A magazine in my waiting room had a test in it that was supposed to tell you if you were nuts or not, so I took that. But all the questions and answers turned out to be jokes. All I got out of it was some big laughs. No actual information.

On the way home, I bought a sanity home testing kit at the store that promised quick sketchy results. You just had to push a strip of colored paper into your mind through your ear. If it turned a certain color, you were crazy. If it turned any other color, you might have a problem. In which case, they recommended you buy more tests. As many tests as the store had. The instructions didn't say what it meant if you lost the colored strip of paper in your head during the test, which is what I did. But I knew that wherever that strip of paper was, and whatever crazy color it had turned, I had a problem.

Now I know what you're thinking: Frank Burly nuts? Get outta here. We weren't born yesterday, most of us. But I knew something was wrong. I had to consult a professional about this. I headed downtown to the Psychiatrist District.

On my way there I was delayed for nearly an hour when a Russian army appeared in front of me, slowly marching across the intersection, with their legs going way up in the air in that funny way they do—like careful Nazis.

"Aw crap," I said, craning my neck to see how long the army was. It was extremely long. I honked my horn, but that did about as much good as it usually does. It made the army go a little faster, but not much. Just when I thought I was never going to get through that intersection, the army suddenly disappeared, like it was never there, and the American flag on a nearby building went back to fifty stars from twenty two.

"There we go!" I said, and continued on my way. These sorts of hallucinations had been happening a lot lately. Everybody had noticed them and wondered about them. But I knew they were nothing to worry about. If something needed to be done about them, our government would do whatever was necessary when the time was right. Nobody is smarter than our government officials. Even I knew that, I thought smugly. Besides, I had problems of my own to take care of.

"I think I'm going nuts, Doc," I said a little while later, as I sat down on Dr. Smirky's couch. "What do you think?"
"What do you think?" he replied.
I repeated my question. "What do you think?"
"What do you think?" he agreed.
After an hour I got fed up with paying good money for "what do you think?" over and over. Call that psychiatry? Because I sure don't. Screw that. I got up to go.
Just then the real Dr. Smirky came in and hung up his coat. I realized I hadn't been talking to him at all! I had thought the guy I was talking to looked a lot like a parrot, but I didn't want to say anything. People are sensitive about their looks. Parrots too, for all I know.
I sat back down and outlined my problem for the doctor. After I had given him all the facts, I asked: "Do you suppose I feel guilty for getting my client killed? And maybe that's why I keep thinking I'm seeing him?"
"No, that's not it."
"It's not?"
"No, that would be too simple. Psychiatry isn't simple, Mr. Burly. You have to go to school for years and years to be a psychiatrist."
"Sure, I know, but..."
"Expensive schools, too. No, Mr. Burly, the human brain is too complicated for simple answers like the one you have suggested. Why, it might be years before you are completely cured."
He tapped out some numbers on his desk calculator, looked at a brochure for a boat, then

tapped out some more numbers. "Nine years," he said.

"Well I only have enough money for this one visit."

He looked disappointed. He put his calculator and boat brochure away. "I see... yes... well, in that case we'll have to keep it simple."

"Good. So what do you think might be causing me to see this ghost?"

"What do you think?"

The psychiatrist frowned. "Somebody shut that parrot up."

A nurse came in and took the parrot away.

"Give it to me straight, Doc. Am I insane?" I asked, worriedly.

"Everyone is a little crazy," he said, soothingly.

I thought about this fact. "That's lucky for you."

"Yes."

"That's money in your pocket."

"Yes." He smiled, in a professional way, but I saw him feeling his pocket to make sure the money was still there.

Over the course of the next hour, Dr. Smirky gave me just about every psychiatric test there was: ink blots, word association tests, everything. We even, at my insistence, did "role reversal", where I pretended I was Dr. Smirky, and got to be the one who looked at the boat brochure, while he had to pretend he was a crap detective with a brain that didn't work.

Throughout my examination he kept telling me to quit pointing at the ghost and saying "there he is, Doc", because he said that wasn't helping with my cure at all. I guess it wasn't, but I mean there he was!

When all the tests had been concluded, the doctor looked them over, then sat me down and explained to me what my problem really was. That's what finally cured me. That talk.

I walked out of the building knowing I would never see another ghost again. Dr. Smirky had explained it all. There was nothing wrong with me. It was everybody else who was screwy. The constant pressure they were unfairly putting on me to quickly solve their cases for them was putting undue pressure on my otherwise fine mind. That was all that was happening here. I felt like slapping those other people silly for causing me so much trouble. They had nearly driven me nuts there for a minute. But now I was cured. And I felt great. I've always wondered why people pay so much money to go to psychiatrists. Now I know. You can't put a price on bullshit like that.

On the way home I saw two ghosts: my regular visitor, and another of my dead clients. They were sitting on the hood of my car, looking through my windshield at me with binoculars, waving at me, and saying: "yoo hoo".

I had to bounce Dr. Smirky around a little, but I finally got all my money back. Cured, my ass. As I left, he told me I was a very sick man, but I said I wasn't falling for that one again. Try it on somebody else.

The patients in his waiting room saw me

coming out counting my money, and I don't think I've ever seen a room full of people so surprised in my life. They hadn't realized you could get your money back on a deal like this. They thought that all of the money they'd spent on being crazy was gone. They crowded into Dr. Smirky's office, loudly demanding their money back too. I didn't stay to see how it all came out, but some of them must have gotten paid back, because for the rest of the day the streets were filled with screaming crowds of crazy people running towards Dr. Smirky's office, gibbering with excitement.

I went back to my office and spent the rest of the afternoon thinking the whole thing over. The simplest solution, I finally decided, was that I wasn't crazy, that there were ghosts, and that that's why I was seeing them. That line of reasoning appealed to me because it was so easy to understand. You don't have to delve into your subconscious or relive your whole lousy childhood to understand that you are seeing something because it's there. That's the kind of simple cause and effect relationship I like. So I decided to go with that.

Now that I was convinced that the ghosts were real, all I had to do was figure out what they wanted with me. That turned out to be easy too. The two ghosts walked in the door and told me themselves.

CHAPTER THREE

Like I said, I'm not exactly comfortable around the supernatural. Because of this, it took the ghosts almost an hour to coax me down from the light fixture, which they finally did with offers of food.

As I nervously ate the sandwich they had promised me—which was surprisingly good. There's something about coming out of a pocket that makes food taste better—they introduced themselves. The short tough looking one said he was Fred C. Cramer, of Indianapolis, Indiana. The wiry one was Ed Brannigan.

"You remember us," said Ed. "We're your dead clients. Fred here got killed in the case you call 'The Great Client Massacre'."

I looked at Fred and tried to recall his part in that case. "Uh... head blown off, right?"

Fred shook his head. "Threshing machine."

Then I remembered. "Oh, yeah. Hi."

Ed continued: "And I hired you to find my wife's real killer, remember that case? The one where you kept finding me?"

I nodded. "Sure. Say, I hope that electric chair didn't hurt much."

"Nah. I kind of enjoyed it. Gave me a buzzy feeling all over. In fact, for awhile there I was thinking of getting one for my house. But then my brain stopped."

"I think I owe both of you men an apology. A sincere apology. One that comes from the heart."

"Nah," said Fred, "you don't owe us nothin'. It was our own fault for hiring such a cheap detective."

"Sure," agreed Ed. "$78.50 for a detective? He's got to stink, right? We deserved everything we got."

"It's nice of you to look at it that way."

"Oh, we're nice ghosts," said Ed

"Very nice," agreed Fred.

They beamed at me. There was an awkward silence. It's hard to know what to say in social situations like this—when you're entertaining people you've recently gotten brutally killed. The etiquette books don't say anything about it. I know. I checked. Finally I said, just to be saying something: "So... er...how have you been? How has death been treating you so far?"

"Being dead's all right," said Fred. "You get into movies free. So you save money that way. And ice skating rinks. Us dead guys can skate all we want for nothing."

"Sure," agreed Ed. "Being dead's a goldmine. Savings everywhere you look. No clothes to buy, no haircuts. No expenses at all. And you have fewer worries, too. For instance, you don't have to worry about your health anymore, or your weight or your sex appeal, because you don't have any of those things."

"Sounds great."

"It is."

"The other clients you got killed say 'hi', by the way," said Fred.

"Oh, good."

The two ghosts seemed friendly enough, but I still couldn't help feeling nervous. They were too transparent, for one thing. I don't like it when I can watch TV through people. Admittedly, it makes scary movies that much scarier, but it makes all the other shows scary too. And that's no good. Make yourself solid if you want to talk to me. That's the way I look at it. That's what I always say. But Ed and Fred couldn't make themselves completely solid. It had something to do with ectoplasm, they told me. That was their answer to just about everything—ectoplasm. I never could find that word in the dictionary. I don't know if they made it up or what. Maybe it's in the dictionary, but it's invisible, I dunno. Anyway, I couldn't find it.

"Well, it sure was swell seeing you fellas again," I said, finishing my sandwich. "Oh, geez, is that the time?"

"You should look at your watch when you say that," said Fred, "not at us."

I looked at my watch and started to say it again.

"Besides," said Ed, "we're not going anyplace."

"You're not?"

"Heck, no. We're sticking with you."

"We came here to help you, pal," explained Fred.

"Help me do what?"

"Everything. Your life's a mess. You're the most unsuccessful man in town."

"That study was flawed," I pointed out.

"But we're going to fix up everything swell for you. Ain't we, Ed?"

"I'll say we are."

"Why?" I asked.

They weren't ready for that question. They had to think for a minute.

"We're trying to win our wings," said Fred, finally.

"I didn't know ghosts had wings."

"Well, we have to win 'em."

"Plus we're trying to win a bar bet," added Ed.

"And we like your face," said Fred. "Is that enough reasons?"

"One more."

They both thought some more. Finally Ed said: "And you need to do 5000 good deeds to get into Heaven, and we've only done 4000."

"4,999" said Fred, correcting him.

"What he said," agreed Ed.

"Yeah, well, the thing is, I don't need any help."

"You let us be the judge of that," said Ed.

"You're not thinking straight right now," said Fred. "On account of you needing our help so much. Isn't that right, Ed?"

"Yeah, he's gone daffy from needing us."

"No, seriously, guys, I appreciate your wanting

to help me, but I will appreciate it even more when you go away."

"Not us," said Ed.

"We're staying," said Fred.

Despite my fear of the supernatural, I was starting to get a little annoyed by these two ghosts.

"Piss off."

"Won't."

I don't like it when people won't do what I say. It happens to me a lot, so I tend to get madder about it than most people do. "Look," I said, "I'll give you two birds just five minutes to get out of here."

After a couple of minutes, I regretted giving them so much time. We were all sitting there looking at our watches. This continued through the full five minutes, and well into the three minute grace period. Finally I lost my patience and tried to pick them up by the scruff of the neck and give them the bum's rush out of my office. But I couldn't get a good grip on them. It was like trying to throw a couple of bad smells out of your office. You can't do it. After several attempts to throw them out had failed, I lost my temper and took a swing at them.

It was like punching nothing at all. No, I take that back. It was like punching my lamp, because my fist went right through them and pulverized a nearby floor lamp. My next punch knocked the couch over. At that point I started swinging wildly, but only managed to destroy all the awards I had ever won, and knock my stamp collection to bits.

I tried kicking them in the ass, but only

succeeded in kicking myself in the face. Fourteen times.

Then I pulled out my gun and shot my office to pieces.

Far from being frightened or angry by this display of violence towards them, the two ghosts seemed to enjoy it, even encourage it. They kept popping up in different parts of the room like shooting gallery targets, as I blazed away, cursing. None of my shots hit their mark, but the bullets did manage to destroy whatever valuable thing was directly behind the ghosts. After ten minutes I didn't have a window or a cherished memento left, and three people who came to complain about the noise were being rushed to the emergency room, complaining about the blood.

Finally I stopped shooting. I hadn't calmed down. I was just out of ammo. I threw my empty gun at them, knocking out my last remaining window.

"Nice shooting," said Ed. "You almost got me there a couple of times."

Fred surveyed the damage to the office. "The first thing we should do to help you get your life back on track is to spruce up this office. You'll never impress clients with an office that looks like this. C'mon, Ed, let's get to work on our good deed."

"Oh boy!"

They both faded away. I didn't try to stop them.

As soon as I was sure they were gone, I picked up the phone and called the cops.

"There's two ghosts bugging me," I told the

desk sergeant. "Get over here quick." Then I gave him my address and tips on the quickest way to get to my office at this time of day. "Better use your siren," I advised. "And you might want to fire your guns in the air as you drive. That will make people get out of your way quicker."

"Ghosts, eh? What exactly do you want us to do about these ghosts, Mr. Burly?"

"I want you to get rid of them for me, obviously," I said. "I want you to serve and protect. Haven't you read the side of your car lately?"

"The thing is, we're a little busy down here at your local police station right now, Mr. Burly," he said, politely. "We have a lot of real crimes to deal with, and unfortunately that means we have less time than we would like to deal with screwballs."

"Well, crap..."

"Tell you what, why don't you come down and file a report—better yet, why not mail us your report? That way the ghosts can help you fill it out. You could even include one of the ghosts in the envelope as evidence, if you like. And the other ghost could be the stamp. Say! That would get rid of your ghost problem, wouldn't it?"

I was beginning to lose patience with this polite, but less than helpful, underling. "Get me your Ghostbusters Unit," I demanded.

"We have no Ghostbusters Unit."

This started a different argument. I said I'd seen the movie personally several times and knew all about the department's celebrated Ghostbusters Unit. He said he'd seen the movie as well, and it was his impression that the

Ghostbusters were a private concern that had nothing to do with the police department. At least, not officially. I said that wasn't the way I remembered the plot of the film. He said I should see the movie again, and pay more attention this time. I said I would when my schedule permitted, but suggested that it would save time if he would just connect me with his Ghostbusters Unit right now. At that point he transferred me to someone else in the department, who spent ten minutes trying to talk me off the ledge he thought I was on. Finally I hung up. I'm not on any ledge.

As I hung up the phone, the two ghosts came in the door carrying a new lamp to replace the one I had punched to pieces, some windows they had found on the floor below, and a large sack of money. Ed handed the money to me. I asked what it was for.

"We figured a guy who runs a cut-rate operation like yours, and dresses and smells like you do must need money pretty bad. So we got you some."

"Hey, thanks. Where'd you get it?"

"Bank."

"We dropped some on the way here," Ed admitted. "But most of it is still in there."

I looked out the window. Policemen were slowly following a trail of money that led from the bank to my building. Fortunately, thanks to passersby picking up souvenirs, and the wind picking up and carrying away even more, the end of the trail had been blotted out just before it reached the door to my building. When they got to the last bill, the policemen had to just stand there scratching their heads, and leaning on my doorknob. So I caught a break there.

"Hey, look you guys," I said, "You're going to get me into trouble if you're not careful. Bank robbery is a crime in this state."

"We're way ahead of you," said Ed. "We left a note at the bank clearing you of any involvement in this. In fact, we left lots of notes."

Fred nodded. "We wrote your name all over the place. Even on the walls. With the guard's blood."

I spent the next twenty minutes trying to hit them with the sack of money. You'd think I would have learned after the first blows went right through them without harming them that the next three hundred would too, but I didn't. I wasn't thinking, I guess.

While I was hammering away at them with the sack, a potential client entered my office.

"Mr. Burly...?"

"I'll be with you in a minute," I said, smashing Ed with the sack, and firing a bullet through Fred's head.

The man stood there watching this for a moment, then slowly backed out the door and down the stairs. The last I heard he was in Ohio, still walking backwards. So there went that job.

Finally, I gave up. I won't say I had learned my lesson, I won't go that far, but I did stop. It had finally gotten through to me that the sack wasn't doing anything. Nothing I had done to get rid of the two ghosts had done anything. I decided that it would be easier to just get rid of me.

So, while they were looking through the closet for other things I could hit them with—they were helpful, I'll give them that—I fled. They wouldn't be able to help someone they couldn't find. Nobody can do that. Nobody's that helpful.

CHAPTER FOUR

They already knew where I lived and where I worked, but I was confident that they didn't know where I hid.

My usual place to do that was in a dumpster in an alley a few blocks from my office. Dumpster Number 7 had always been a good spot for me. People would find me in Dumpster Number 3. Easy. Might as well have been sitting on top of it. And they'd usually drag me out of the other dumpsters after a half hour or so. But they never found me in good old Number 7. It was lucky for some reason. I had hidden there so often in recent months, I was starting to get credit card offers there. And that's not a joke. Credit card companies don't send you offers like that just to be funny. They want your business too much to make jokes about it.

Five minutes after I had arrived at Number 7, and gotten myself settled in, and was looking around for something to eat, I noticed I wasn't alone.

"This place is even worse than your other place," said Ed.

"We're going to have to fix this up too," said Fred, with a trace of annoyance.

They began discussing ways to spiff up the interior of the dumpster. Fred thought a velvet painting on the lid might help. Ed thought a couple of throw rugs were the key. As for the rats, Fred was for throwing them out, while Ed felt brushing their teeth would be enough.

I didn't hang around to take part in this discussion. I was off and running again.

Over the next week, I guess I must have hidden just about everywhere you can hide in Central City: In out-of-the-way motels, where the bellhops who carried my bags up to my room turned out to be Ed and Fred; in hobo jungles, where the mulligan stew kept saying "Hi, Burly"; in Dumpster Number 7 again, where there wasn't room enough for all three of us to sleep—we finally had to hook two dumpsters together; in the city sewer system where I hid under an unusually large turd, which turned out to be Fred; and so on—from one great hiding place to another. Did you know there's a small rusted out hole half way up the suspension bridge over the Central City River that you can wedge yourself into? There is. And did you know there are ghosts in there waiting for you? There are.

I tried everything to throw the ghosts off my trail. I even tried changing my appearance. But the cut-rate plastic surgeon I went to didn't do anything except put both my eyes on the same side of my face. That didn't fool anybody. Just grossed them out.

Everywhere I went, Ed and Fred were always there too. Usually they got there around the same time I did, or a little before. Sometimes they showed up later, complaining about the traffic. But whenever they found me, they always immediately went to work, doing everything they could to make my life better.

The first thing they did was make sure that money was no problem for me in my travels. When I walked down the street, everyone around me had their pockets picked, with the money miraculously floating through the air and into my pocket. Sometimes cash registers would float out of nearby shops into my waiting arms. And armored cars tried to follow me home. I like money as much as the next guy, but this way of getting it made me uncomfortable. I knew it didn't look good.

People kept asking me for explanations for these strange events. They wanted to know how they happened—the physics behind them. I told them I didn't owe them any explanations. They said no, but they'd appreciate an explanation just the same.

Finally I figured out a way to stop the constant questioning. While they were still gaping at the sight of their life savings floating slowly into my hand, I'd instantly demand: "How did that happen? What did you just do there?" Get the jump on them, see? Take control of the situation. They'd stammer out something like "Well I don't know." And I'd say "Well you better figure it out, because it looks pretty strange to me." Usually they'd just mumble something about sunspots or something and hurry away. So that's how I solved that problem.

Another problem that the ghosts inadvertently caused me was when they tried to get my detective business some free publicity.

"Look," said Fred, handing me a copy of the Central City Times, as he and Ed were helping me hide from them under a toll road, "we got your name in the paper. That's got to be good for business."

I looked at the paper. It had a small picture of me, along with the caption: "Local Detective Suspected In String Of Robberies." There were other articles about me on the inside pages, most of them in connection with hold-ups, kidnappings, burglaries, and other major crimes. Practically the whole paper was about me. Okay, publicity is good, I acknowledge that, but I was worried this was the wrong kind of publicity I was getting. But try to explain that to Ed and Fred.

My two ghostly helpers even took a crack at pepping up my love life for me.

"You seem to lead a pretty lonely existence here behind this mailbox," said Ed, with concern, after he had found me hiding from him behind it. "That doesn't seem right, a big good-looking guy like you." He looked around the street for a moment, then spotted what he was looking for. "You like that woman?" He pointed at a tall blonde crossing the street.

"Well, sure!"
"We'll get her for you."
"Say, hang on now..."

Ed and Fred faded from sight. Then, working invisibly, the two ghosts tipped my hat at the woman, filled the air with wolf whistles, rearranged my face into a leer, and unzipped my pants. The woman walked over to a nearby policeman, talked to him for a moment and pointed at me. As he began walking towards me, I began tipping my hat at the policeman, my pants zipper going rapidly up and down. The only "date" I ended up getting was a "date" in "court". My ghostly friends didn't seem to realize it, but they were causing me a lot of trouble with these stunts of theirs. They were hurting me more than they were helping me.

All the time I was on the run from the ghosts, I kept trying everything I could think of to get rid of them once and for all.

I tried dynamite, flamethrowers, hand grenades—I guess I must have blown up about a quarter of my neighborhood before it was all over. But none of the blasts bothered the ghosts in the slightest. I think they kind of liked them, if the word "wheee!" is any indication.

I called in ghost hunters and said "There's two", but they just got scared and ran away. Some ghost hunters.

I tried nailing the ghosts in a box and shipping them to someone I didn't like, but all I got out of that was a phone call from the guy saying "Hey, thanks for the empty box".

When I couldn't think of anything else to try—when I was drawing a blank—Ed and Fred quickly chipped in with some ideas of their own.

"Try spraying us with acid," suggested Fred.

"Does that work?"

"No."

"Why did you suggest it then?"

"We don't like seeing you running out of ideas like this. We want to help."

"Oh, I see."

"How about dropping an A-bomb on us?" said Ed. "The flying wing could carry it."

I looked at him dubiously. "Any chance of that working?"

"Nope."

"Maybe a signed petition would work," suggested Fred. "Ever think of that?"

"I'll sign that petition right now!" said Ed, enthusiastically.

Finally, after the A-bomb from the flying wing thing didn't work, I gave up. I couldn't hide from them. I couldn't destroy them. I couldn't do anything.

I headed back to my office. At least I could do that. At least I could head places.

When I got there I noticed that my office looked a lot better than it usually did. The ghosts had apparently been working on it all the time I was away. Not only was it decorated nicely, with all sorts of velvet paintings and throw rugs, it was jam-packed with all sorts of detective stuff I'd always wanted, but could never afford: an FBI-quality surveillance setup so I could do my stakeouts in the comfort of my own home or office; a real professional magnifying glass—one of those glass jobs, not the cheap plastic things I always use; an electronic footprint database that had every foot in America in it; Mickey Mantle Model Handcuffs; everything. Most of it wasn't new—it had been stolen from other detectives in the area—but it was still serviceable.

And I noticed my waiting room was filled with dozens of new clients, all bound and gagged and ready to hire me, all apparently kidnapped from other detectives' offices.

I started to rethink my position on all this. What exactly is wrong with people helping you? When did that become a bad thing? What am I, nuts?

The capper was when my girl came to visit later that day.

"Are these your friends, Franklin?" she asked when she saw Ed and Fred bringing in the next bound and gagged client for me to interview.

"No."

The ghosts looked hurt. "We're not?" asked Fred.

"Well..." I thought of all the great new stuff they'd just gotten me, "...in a way, maybe, but..."

She looked at them and sniffed. She plainly didn't think much of my new friends.

I haven't told you about my girl, Myrna, because... well... I'm kind of embarrassed about her. She looks awful. And her language would embarrass a sailor. And I don't mean a regular sailor. I mean one of those sailors who don't embarrass easily. But, beggars can't be choosers, the Good Book says. That's how I ended up with Myrna.

Anyway, by the end of the day the two ghosts had managed to inadvertently insult her more than I had in my entire life. They called her a "broad", engaged in playful wrestling matches with her, poked her in the ass with the wrong fork during dinner, yelled obscenities up her dress, and kept advising her, as one friend to another, to take the mask off because Halloween was over.

Finally she had had enough. She stormed out, throwing her engagement ring back at me and saying she would never darken my door again. Hey, I thought, these ghosts are all right. I'd been trying to get her to do that for a year. Not only that, but it was a previous boyfriend who had bought that ring for her, not me. So I was up one ring on the deal.

I decided right then and there that I had been a fool to resist. A couple of ghosts were probably just what I had needed all along.

"From now on, we're partners," I said, shaking their clammy hands. "Welcome to the firm."

They looked at me with surprise, and, unless I imagined it, a little dismay.

I got on the phone to order some little desks for them.

CHAPTER FIVE

I don't know how I lived all those years without slaves. I honestly don't. It's a little thing, but it makes all the difference if you want to live the good life.

From the moment I got the Spirit World working for me, my life became a breeze. Anything I wanted just floated into my hands. Things I didn't want anymore were quickly taken away. And if anything got in my path, it was violently hurled aside by an unseen force.

"Scare that guy," I would say regally as I walked down Main Street with the fellas. "Bring me a beer. Knock those children out of my way." And all my wishes instantly came true. It was wonderful. I was finally living the kind of life Frank Burly deserved. Finally life was fair.

I had Ed and Fred doing everything for me: doing all the legwork on my cases, making sure my clients paid their bills on time, painting my house the "Color of the Week", preparing my meals and snacks, even bathing and dressing me and my clients. You name something a slave can do for his beloved master and they were doing it for me.

"No," I would say, "I think the couch would look better over there. No, second thoughts, back where it was is better. Tell you what, why don't you keep moving it back and forth like that. I like that. The constant movement appeals to my aesthetic sense."

And they had to do it, because it was helping me, see? Of course, they did their share of griping. All slaves do that, I'm told. But every time they complained, all I had to do was remind them of why they were here.

"Hey, listen, Burly..." Ed would begin, after I had told him to put in a new lawn, for example— the one he had put in last week wasn't new anymore. It had birds on it now—but before he could get any farther I would stifle his complaints with a wave of my hand.

"You want to help me, don't you?"

"Well, sure, but..."

"You want to do your good deed."

"Yeah."

"You still like my face as much as ever, don't you?"

"I guess."

"Well my face needs a new lawn. So let's get going. Chop chop."

Life had become a dream for me. Nothing was hard. Everything was easy. I didn't even have to do my own walking anymore. My legs were moved up and down for me, as I strolled down the street, while I relaxed and ate grapes. I didn't even have to buy the grapes. They were stolen for me. Nothing I wanted in life was denied me. If I coveted my neighbor's ass, I got it.

Of course there's more to be gained from Heavenly Help than mere creature comforts. There's money to be made, too.

In one weekend at a gambling casino, thanks to a little invisible help, I won $428. I probably would have won more, but I only was betting one dollar chips. Better safe than sorry, I always say. And I probably shouldn't have changed some of my bets at the last second when I got one of those sudden wild hunches of mine. Those hunch bets all turned out to be losers. But it wasn't the amount of money I had won that mattered, it was the feeling that I hadn't earned any of it. There's no better feeling than that.

The best part of all this was that I knew it would never end. All good things must come to an end for other people. For the suckers. But not for me. The rules didn't apply to me anymore. I was the King of the Spirit World. Make way for the King.

Then one evening it all ended.

I had just had one of the best days of my life. You know those kinds of days where everything just goes right? Where everybody else's tax refunds end up in your mailbox? Where your business rivals spend the whole day stuck in elevators and all their clients have to come to you? Where the horse you bet on is the only horse in the race that doesn't get spooked by something? Where the IRS man who's coming to talk to you about stolen tax refunds meets with, like, an accident? You know days like that? Well it was one of those kinds of days for me.

I was sitting in my easy chair, smoking a fine Cuban cigar that had been yanked out of Castro's mouth for me, while my little helpers, worn out from their day's exertions on my behalf, were tiredly soaking their feet in ghostly buckets of water.

"Whose idea was it to be nice to him?" asked Fred.

"It was my idea," replied Ed, pouring more hot water into the bucket, "and it made sense in theory. Piles of sense."

"Well, look where we are now. Look where your precious theories have gotten us. He's got us working our butts off here, and his life is better than it was, not worse."

I had been listening to this exchange. I tapped my foot. "Those clippings won't paste themselves into my scrapbook by themselves," I said.

"Screw your scrapbook," said Fred.

I was stunned. Nobody talks that way about my scrapbook. What had gotten into my slaves today? Griping I could understand. I've been known to gripe myself from time to time, when nothing else would work, but this bordered on insubordination. I rose up to my full height, towering a full ¼ inch higher than before. My back really hurts when I do that, but it's worth it because I'm definitely taller.

"What's that?" I demanded.

They rose up to their full heights and looked

at me in a way that reminded me of how afraid of ghosts I am. They had never looked at me like that before.

"Hey, what's the matter with you guys?" I asked, looking worriedly from one malevolent face to the other, "Are you sick or something?"

"We're sick all right," said Ed, grimly. "We're sick of you."

"Me? How could you be sick of me? I'm your pal! Your buddy! Your hero! You came here all the way from Heaven just to help me."

"No we didn't."

"Huh?"

"What kind of saps do you think we are?" asked Fred.

"Well..." I began. Then I stopped. I wasn't sure calling them any kind of saps would be a good idea right now. So I didn't say any more. I just waited for them to say something.

That's when they told me the truth. They said they hadn't come here to help me at all. Their plan had been to pretend to be helping me, but in doing so to screw up my life horribly. By now, they said, the cops should have arrested me on dozens of charges, from intimidation to murder. My friends should have abandoned me for acting so haunted all the time (I had fooled them there. I have no friends), and my business should have folded for the same reason. They didn't know what had gone wrong. Maybe their plan had failed because it was too clever. (That's why my plans fail too!) Anyway, they were through being clever, they told me. Their new plan was to just wreck my life as quickly as possible and get the heck out of here.

I couldn't fathom any of this. It didn't make sense to me.

"But why are you doing this? What have I ever done to you?"

"Well, you killed us," said Fred.

"And I apologized, didn't I? And you said... well, I forget exactly what you said... but I'm pretty sure you accepted my apology. Besides, you said you liked being dead."

"We don't," said Fred. "It stinks."

"But the ice skating..."

"It stinks, I tell you. Never mind about the ice skating. That's not important."

"Because of you, we're doomed to wander the Earth as ghosts for the next thirty years," said Ed.

"I don't understand," I said.

They made some cheap cracks about me not understanding anything—the usual stuff. I get it all the time. It doesn't even bother me anymore—then they gave me a short course in how the afterlife works.

They said that ghosts are people who aren't supposed to be dead yet. Their time isn't up. So there's no place for them in the afterlife yet. Their clouds aren't ready—they have to be painted or fumigated or something. I wasn't clear on that point. Anyway they're not ready. So people who die earlier than scheduled have to hang around here and wait. Ed and Fred said they were going to be stuck here until 2038, with nothing to do. That's why they were so steamed at me.

I was stunned. I didn't know what to say. I handed them another scrapbook and told them to get pasting. They refused. They said they weren't my little helpers anymore. They were my enemies now.

I tried to smooth things over. I made a little speech. I said that whatever our differences had been in the past, no matter who killed who, I was confident that... hey, where did they go?

I looked out in the corridor to see if maybe they were out there spit-shining my door, like I had told them to do earlier that day. They weren't. Then I checked the elevator to see if maybe they were in there installing that shower I wanted. They weren't there either. I started to get the feeling that my little speech hadn't smoothed things over as well as I'd hoped.

It hadn't.

From that moment forward, Ed and Fred did everything they could to get me in as much trouble as possible. Every time I walked past a policeman, for example, I would hear him say: "Hey, who kicked me in the ass?" And then two voices, neither one of them mine, would say: "I did it. Me. Frank Burly". This always doubly pissed off the cops. Not only was I not showing proper respect for a police officer, I wasn't even bothering to sync up my words with my mouth. There's no law about that, of course, but the police don't like it.

And every time I walked past a building it suddenly caught fire. When the fire department arrived, my arms were always full of gas cans, political manifestos, and suicide notes. And the only explanation I could think of to give them was a weak laugh—a laugh that got weaker the longer they looked at me. Each of these fires was deemed "suspicious". And so was I.

Dead bodies began appearing all around me: all over my property, in my bed, in my office, and leaning up against the side of my house. I wasn't sure whether Ed and Fred were killing all of these people or just digging them up somewhere, but it didn't really matter, from my point of view. Either way, it made me look bad.

"What's all this then?" a policeman would say, gazing at all the corpses on my roof.

"This isn't what it looks like, officer," I would say.

"It better not be."

"It's just a gag."

"Gag, eh?"

"Yes."

"It needs some work."

"I realize that officer."

"It's not funny, for one thing."

"No, I suppose not. And yet…"

"And it doesn't seem to be about anything."

"It needs work all right."

"Got any more gags like this?"

"Not at this time, officer."

"Good."

I had a hard time moving all the corpses off of my property, because most of the time I couldn't find my car. It was usually roaming around Central City by itself, with the words "Frank Burly

Special" painted on the side, causing wrecks, knocking over pedestrians, and double parking in front of the police station and leaning on its horn. It was racking up over 400 traffic violations a day for me. The cops ran out of ticket books at one point. They had to order some more.

I probably should have been arrested right away for all of these crimes I seemed to be committing, but I wasn't.

Fortunately for me, our new police chief was a very methodical man. He was tired of losing cases in court because a piece of evidence was thrown out for being bullshit. He insisted that his men collect every possible shred of evidence before an arrest was made. This backfired in my case, because I was giving the police more evidence against me every day. Better evidence, too. No policeman in his right mind would want to go to trial without all this great new evidence I was giving him. So if I didn't stop, or at least slow down, they'd never catch up.

They did ask me to come downtown frequently to discuss all the crimes that were being committed in Central City, and my possible starring role in them. In fact, I was at the police station so often they gave me a reserved parking place next to the entrance. It was a better spot than the chief had. But they weren't ready to arrest me yet. Just a little more evidence. They had to make sure. They knew if they blew this one they would be laughed out of the law business.

Another reason the police hadn't arrested me

yet was that they were being kept very busy looking into all of the hallucinations that had been occurring around town; landmarks would disappear and then reappear again, sometimes looking slightly different; streets would suddenly be pointing in different directions and be named for people no one had ever heard of, like "William Howard Taft"; statues in city parks would suddenly be of different guys, or of the same guy riding a different horse, or the same horse with an entirely different name; and nuclear bomb clouds sprang up everywhere, then faded away, leaving no damage that anyone could see.

Nobody seemed to know what to make of all these hallucinations, but since they didn't appear to be dangerous, no one was too concerned. But the police had to investigate them all, which left them with less time than they would have liked to investigate what appeared to be the only really dangerous thing in Central City right then—me.

I was hiding the evidence of my crimes as fast as I discovered them, but it seemed like a losing battle. My garage was full, I'd dug as many holes in my yard as I dared—my gardener was threatening to learn English and quit—and I was renting storage areas all over the city and packing them full of corpses, stolen money, kidnap victims, drug paraphernalia, and bogus tax returns.

Then one day I went too far. That was the day the cops found Amelia Earhart in the trunk of my car. And that's when all hell broke loose.

Even though it was a little the worse for wear,

it was definitely Amelia Earhart's body. It was wearing a vintage leather flying helmet, one hand held the keys to a 1932 Lockheed Electra, and tags on the body said "If Found Return To Current U.S. Government" and "This End Up", which for some reason was on both ends.

This didn't look good for me. I would have to answer a lot of tough, searching questions about this one. This wasn't just any body. This body was important. This body's face was on postage stamps. Of course, it wasn't all bad. Thanks to the publicity I would be getting for my monstrous crime, I'd probably get some new clients out of this. People who wanted me to find their pilots, for example. But I still didn't like the looks of it.

The police chief decided it was time to make his move. There was no point in delaying my arrest any longer. I would never be more guilty-looking than this. No one ever would. If he couldn't get a conviction against me now, with the mountains of evidence he already had, plus this spectacular new Earhart thing, he wasn't the chief of police he thought he was.

Ed and Fred were in the crowd of onlookers as I was resisting arrest. When I spotted them I called out: "Hey, if you still want to help me why don't you kill some of these cops?"

One of the cops frowned. "That's enough of that now."

CHAPTER SIX

I've never had much luck in courtrooms. I'm always guilty, is one problem. The deck is pretty stacked against us guilty guys right from the start. It's like they don't want to give us a fair trial. Everyone else has an even shot of beating the rap, but not us, oh no. We get railroaded. And all because we are guilty, and everybody can prove it. I saw there was an extra large amount of evidence against me this time—even I said "Jesus!" when I saw it all—so I wasn't very confident going into this one.

The lawyer the court assigned to represent me in this case didn't inspire much confidence either. Henry Loser, his name was. Talk about a bad omen! I asked him if it was pronounced "Loo-zay" or something French like that, but he said no, it was "Loser". He said it was an Old English name, from back in the days when they gave you a surname based on what you did. I asked him if he wanted to discuss the case with me, maybe get my side of it, but he just said "What's the point?" and I said "You got that right". We didn't talk much after that.

My trial was a bit of a three ring circus right from the start. Not only was I there, (I heard some jurors mutter "Here comes trouble" when I arrived), but the courtroom was filled to capacity with conspiracy buffs, fans of unsolved crimes, aviation experts, and other assorted nuts. Some of the more enthusiastic spectators came to the trial dressed up to look like Amelia Earhart. A few were dressed up to look like me. Adding an ominous note to the proceedings was a small group of grim looking men in unfashionable black suits watching the trial from the rear of the courtroom and occasionally talking in low voices into 1979 vintage cell phones. I didn't like the look of them. Of course, I didn't like any of this.

When it was time for the trial to begin, the judge cleared his throat and addressed me: "So, Mr. Burly, according to the statement you gave the police, a couple of..." He looked at a transcript of my statement. "...little pricks named Ed and Fred put the body of Amelia Earhart in your car?"

"That is correct, Your Honor," I replied. "Fred Cramer and Ed Brannigan. B-r-a-double n..."

"And you had nothing to do with it?"

"Nothing at all, Your Honor. I am completely innocent."

I felt unseen fingers pull the sides of my mouth out into a huge uncomfortable smile. The judge seemed to back up a little in his chair, then stared at me for a moment before resuming.

"And where are these..." He looked at the

transcript again. "...little pricks? Why aren't they in the courtroom?"

"They are, Your Honor," I said. "Right behind me, with their fingers in my mouth."

He stared at me again. "I see no one behind you."

"No, sir, they cannot be seen."

"Why not?"

"Ectoplasm."

"What?"

"They are ghosts, Your Honor."

This threw the courtroom into an uproar. Everyone began talking at once. As the excitement grew, one of the spectators who was dressed as Amelia Earhart began running around the room with his arms stretched out as if he was flying. Most of the ones who were dressed like me hid their faces in their hands.

While the judge tried to restore order, I looked around for Ed and Fred. They were still invisible, but I could sense they were nearby because one of their fingers was still in my mouth. Then two voices started whispering in my ear.

"Hi, Burly," said Fred.

"We thought it over and decided we haven't been fair to you," said Ed. "You didn't try to get us killed. If you had, you would have screwed it up. We would have won the lottery or something instead."

"That's right," I agreed.

"Or been elected Pope," said Fred.

"Sure."

"We'd both be lottery-winning Popes by now."

"Well that's what I've been trying to tell you."

"So we're sorry for all the trouble we've caused you. Really sorry," said Ed. "Fred here can't sleep."

"I tossed and turned all night," said Fred. "I'm gripped with remorse. Want to see?"

"No."

"We'll make it up to you though," promised Ed. "Don't worry, we'll help you beat this rap."

"Good. It's about time somebody started helping me around here. All these courtroom jerks are..."

I suddenly noticed that all the furor in the courtroom had subsided and everyone was staring at me. I guess it must have looked kind of crazy, me talking to the air like that, and making plans with it, and giving it high fives.

It looked even crazier moments later when my hair started combing itself, dust started being patted off my jacket, and invisible hands started brushing my teeth. I looked a lot more presentable that way, I guess, but, like I said, it looked crazy too.

"Ghosts, eh?" said the judge, doing his best, for the dignity of the court, to ignore the fact that some unseen force was ironing my shirt, and my head was trying on different hats by itself.

I spit out some toothpaste. "Yes, Your Honor, ghosts."

The judge leafed through my statement again. "Where did these 'ghosts' say they got the body of Miss Earhart?"

There was some hurried whispering in my ear.

"Uh... they found it on the grounds of the

Imperial Palace in Tokyo, Your Honor," I said, "behind a really old bush."

There was a rumble of excitement from the spectators in the courtroom. The dark-suited men in the back of the room stiffened. The judge banged his gavel until the courtroom was silent again.

"And... um... did these ghosts tell you how they knew the body was there?"

There was more hurried whispering in my ear.

"Er... as I understand it, they play tennis with the ghost of Miss Earhart every Tuesday. She told them where her body was hidden during one of these games. And, I don't know if it's important or not, but according to them they beat her pants off regularly."

"It's not important."

"The jury will disregard the part about Miss Earhart's pants," I announced.

"I will instruct the jury, Mr. Burly."

I shrugged. "Fine."

I noticed that the spectators in the courtroom were beginning to look at me with narrowing eyes. As much as they wanted to believe anything anybody ever said to them—the screwier the better as far as they were concerned—apparently my story wasn't quite ringing true to them. Only the men in the black suits in the back of the courtroom seemed to be taking me seriously now. They were taking notes, making phone calls and eyeing me coldly.

"If what you say is true," said the judge, dryly, "this appears to solve a very old mystery."

"Solving mysteries is my business, Your Honor," I said, swaggering a little, giving a small wave to the jury, and winking at the cops.

At this point, there was more excited whispering in my ear. I listened for a moment, then addressed the judge.

"Your Honor, I can also solve the Judge Crater disappearance mystery at this time, if the court pleases."

"Oh?"

"Yes. He's also in the trunk of my car. Farther back than the other corpse. Behind the spare tire."

This created an even bigger sensation in the courtroom. The trial was recessed for an hour while my impounded car was checked out by the police again. They tore the whole thing apart, right down to the axles, then they opened the trunk. The body of Judge Crater was found exactly where Ed and Fred said it would be. It was right there behind the spare tire, right under Ambrose Bierce. The afternoon papers screamed the headline: "More Bodies Found In Death Trunk!"

I was hoping that solving all these age-old mysteries would help me out in my trial, make the law see me in a more favorable light. Like some kind of an Indiana Jones type character. Instead, I just seemed like a nut who had a graveyard in his car.

My trial continued throughout the rest of the afternoon, but I won't bore you with all the details. It was just a lot of irrefutable evidence being brought out against me, and the prosecutor making a monkey out of me on the stand, and the judge asking my lawyer if he wanted to object to anything, and my lawyer replying "Why bother?" and "Leave me alone". And all of it was punctuated with strange looking actions on my part: my pants pressing themselves, my eyebrows being plucked by an unseen hand until I looked like a movie star, key evidence mysteriously floating into my inside coat pocket and having to be retrieved by the bailiff, the jury members being prodded in the ribs by unseen elbows when I accidentally got off a good crack, and so on.

At the conclusion of the trial, the jury only got halfway up out of their seats before they had finished their deliberations and started sitting back down again. They wouldn't look at me, which I took as a good sign.

The foreman stood up. "We find the defendant, Frank Burly, innocent..."

There was an explosion of stunned cursing behind me. "This is bullshit!" the voice howled.

"What did you say, Mr. Burly?" asked the judge.

"Nothing, Your Honor."

"Did you say something was bullshit?"

"No, Your Honor."

"Then may we proceed?"

"Please."

The judge nodded to the jury foreman, who resumed reading the verdict.

"We find the defendant, Frank Burly, innocent by reason of insanity."

"You see," I told the cop who had arrested me, "I told you I was innocent."

As I was being led out of the courtroom in a straightjacket, I looked back and saw Ed and Fred, now fully materialized, shaking hands with the horrified jury foreman, and beaming over at me. It suddenly occurred to me that they hadn't been here to help me at all! They had just shown up to make sure my trial went badly. And I had fallen for it.

When they began fading away, the last thing that disappeared were their two malicious smiles, which hung there in the air for a few moments after they were gone. I don't know what made me madder, ruining my life or plagiarizing Alice in Wonderland like that. Ruining my life, I guess.

CHAPTER SEVEN

The asylum they put me in had been originally called the Central City Loony Bin, but in the 1970's the name was changed to J.J.Nutball's Gibber Palace, a trendy name designed to get more young people into the place. The advertising man who came up with the name said that it was "Now", and would increase traffic and generate added revenue "Soon", but it never did. A few more young people did go insane, but some of the older nuts were turned off by the name change and got better. Financially, it ended up being pretty much a wash.

Recently the name had been changed back, but, in a nod to political correctness, it was now called the Central City Special Bin. Inmates were treated as if they were normal fully functioning members of society, who just needed a special bin to live in. There was nothing "wrong" with them. They were the same as everybody else. This modern way of looking at the problem meant the staff didn't have to treat their patients, or cure them, or even watch them particularly. Just chuck them in their Special Place, and slam and lock their Special Door. Made things a lot easier for the staff. Pretty smart, I thought.

When I was checked into the place, they took away my street clothes and gave me a pair of special coveralls to wear. These had no sharp zippers that might pinch my skin, or any buttons that I could accidentally choke on—no way to get them off at all. And they were a bright orange color, so I would be in a good orangey mood whenever I looked down at what I was wearing, and would be less likely to do something "special". Despite all these precautions, I noticed they let me keep my belt.

"Aren't you going to take away my belt so I won't hang myself?" I asked.

"Usually we do," said a member of the staff, "but we're a little overcrowded right now. So it's either build another wing or let the inmates keep their belts. If you lose yours, you can get another one from the Belt Lady."

"You might want a second belt anyway," chimed in another staffer. "One to hang yourself with, the other to keep your pants up while you hang."

That seemed like a good idea. I picked out a couple of good strong looking belts. I wasn't planning on hanging myself, but if I did, I wanted to make sure I hung there with dignity.

I was ushered into a large room filled with inmates who were dressed exactly like myself—though a few wore old faded baseball caps that said "I'm Nuts For The Gibber Palace".

No one took any notice of me when I came in. They didn't seem to be taking any notice of anything. They were just sitting and staring at nothing, as if the world around them had ceased to exist. I asked the nurse if I could have whatever drug they were having. I could use a rest like that. She said it had already been sprinkled on the candy bar I was eating, and the finger I was picking my nose with. I said good.

Once the door to the outside world had slammed shut behind me, and I was alone with the other special people like myself, I relaxed for the first time in months, maybe years. Now, finally, the pressure was off. The world can't expect much of you if you're locked away in a loony bin. Life is unfair, but it's not that unfair. No one can expect you to be a success anymore, or keep up with the current trends, or even keep your pants up. You don't have to pay your taxes, plan for the future, or explain why you just yelled "SMEM!" so loud. You're set. It's like being royalty. I felt like King George III.

I picked out a nice comfortable looking chair, turned it so it was pointed away from the real world, then sat down and began my staring. There was a humorous sign on the wall near me that said "You Don't Have To Be Crazy To Be Here, But It Helps". It was funny because it was true, like... I dunno... I was going to say the Lincoln Assassination, but I guess that's not a good example. The Lincoln Assassination is true, but it's not funny enough. I'll think of a better example later. Anyway, you know what I'm driving at.

I was still laughing at how true the sign was when Ed and Fred showed up to gloat. They really gave me the horselaugh, letting me know that this is what happens to people who cause them trouble. People who cause them trouble get it in the neck. They get theirs. Their ass is grass. And so on.

They were quite enjoying themselves, but they didn't end up staying long. After awhile, they began to feel uncomfortable there. They didn't like being in a place where everybody could see them all the time, even when they were invisible. They weren't used to eyes following them wherever they went. So finally they cut their gloating short, and left. We all watched them go, then I went back to my staring. I was getting a little behind in that.

After awhile, I started taking an interest in things, despite myself. The other people in the room began to fascinate me. Special was the right word for them.

They didn't think of themselves as people with mental problems. They thought they were a lot more interesting than that. Some thought they could fly, some thought they could walk up the walls, some thought they could transform their bodies to appear to be something else, like extension ladders, or race cars, or—if a nurse was coming—mental patients. They all thought they could do something amazing. What was fascinating about them was that, as near as I could tell, they really could do those things. I asked the nurse if these delusions were why they were committed to the asylum, pointing out that the delusions seemed very real to me. Three patients were walking on the ceiling right now. And one of them who claimed to be the rightful King of Spain was, in fact, wearing what looked like a very valuable crown. And there were Spaniards outside his window waiting for him to tell them what to do.

"Oh, no, they can do everything they say," she said. "They're crazy, not liars."

I was getting confused. "But... if they can do those things..."

She interrupted me: "Sounds like someone needs more 'Head On A Pole'."

"Yes, please."

After she had given me my medicine, I tried to get back to my staring, but it was difficult. I was starting to get a little bored with it. You can only stare at something for so long before it starts looking the same.

When I could get some of the other inmates alone, out of earshot of the nurses, I asked them when the big escape was going to be. I knew a big escape was being planned, because it always is in places like this. Television has taught us that much. They said it was set for tonight. They said they had been waiting for a big stupid guy who could act as the muscle for their operation. And I had finally showed up. Just when they were starting to think I wouldn't. I said I wasn't stupid. I was methodical. To the point of stupidity. But I was pretty big. Would I do? They said I was perfect.

"We've got our big stupid guy," one of them said, rubbing his hands with satisfaction.

"What do you want me to do?" I asked.

"You stand in the middle of the room and fight everybody while we escape."

"And then I escape."

"What?"

"After you escape, then I do."

"Er... yes, that's right."

"Because that's the way it would have to work if it was going to be fair."

"Uh... absolutely. You escape too."

"Fine."

Late that night the asylum was thrown into an uproar. One of the institution's Special Residents had gone insane! All the nurses, doctors, and administrators came rushing into the main room to see me standing there swinging belts around and yelling and gibbering like a madman.

The first nurse to reach me tried to calm me down with a hypodermic needle and a few soothing words. I decked her. The next one came at me with a blackjack. I decked her too.

"Gibber!" I yelled, doing my best to imitate someone who was not just special, but really special—specialer than a fruitcake, "Gibber gibber yell yell!"

More nurses and doctors tried to restrain me, but I knocked them over as fast as they arrived. The nuts were right about me. I was perfect for this job. It's too bad it was just a one day deal. I could probably have made a nice living doing this.

While I was keeping the staff busy, and security men were being summoned from their normal stations outside to lend a hand in subduing me, inmates started going over the wall by the dozens.

Some flew out, chattering like helicopters, others bounced over the wall like the pogo sticks they thought they were, and one who thought he was Lindbergh flew out in an airplane he'd made out of toilet paper rolls that thought they were airplane parts. One guy with a split personality escaped five different ways. Though I'm told they later found two of him.

I was right behind the last of the inmates, with two nurses still clinging doggedly to me, one trying to take my temperature to find out what was wrong with me, and the other trying to tell me a bedtime story so I'd go to sleep.

I shook them off and grabbed the long plasticine arm of an inmate who thought he was a comic book hero, and was dragged up and over the wall to freedom.

Once we were outside, I immediately split off from the others. I figured I could do better on my own, since I was sane and they were not. So when they headed north, I went south. I don't know what happened to the rest of them, but I know at least one of them got away clean, because I later saw him in the news, breaking the sound barrier, with his face. So he did all right. But I didn't.

Just as I got clear of the other inmates, and took my first step south, a hand came down on my shoulder. I looked up. It was a G-Man. And he had a gun.

CHAPTER EIGHT

I was taken to a large ominous government facility out near the edge of town. Central City had outbid Cuba for it. Its purpose was vague, but the money it generated for the local economy was real, and that's all the City Council cared about, so there were no investigations by the city into the weird noises or diabolical laughter that came out of the facility. The people who lived in the neighborhood complained about all the noise—and about the annoying "secret" smell that belched out of the facility's smokestacks day and night, a smell that no one could identify exactly, but no one liked—but nothing was ever done to look into these complaints. A lot of City Council members' salaries were paid for indirectly by that facility, and no one wanted to jeopardize their salaries. Nobody's that stupid.

Beyond the heavily guarded main gate was nearly an acre of mixed barbed wire and dogs. Then more gates, with a dog on each one.

The main building was even more secure. There were guards at every door, on both sides.

You couldn't open a door without hitting a guard's head with it. The swinging doors usually got both of them. So the guards were all in a mean mood. After awhile, my escorts stopped letting me open the doors. They made me walk in the middle of the group.

I was taken to the office of the man running the facility, a Mr. Albert Conklin. He was a thin white-haired, pleasant looking old duffer, but in my experience nothing about the government is pleasant—except for maybe the stamps. Some of the stamps are quite nice. So I wasn't fooled by appearances. I expected him to be trouble. And he was.

Before he could say anything to me, I asked him a question—a question I ask everyone I meet for the first time: "Are you going to kill me?"

"Killing you isn't enough, I'm afraid."

"Oh. That's too bad. Are you sure, because…"

"Oh we're quite sure. You've caused too many problems already. Just stopping you from causing any more won't do us any good. It won't get rid of the ones you've already caused."

"No, I can see that now." I thought for a minute. "Wait, I think I thought of a way where killing me would be enough."

"It's too late now."

I made a face.

"What are you so happy about?"

"Oh. Sorry. Wrong face."

I made another face.

"You're right to look worried, Mr. Burly, because…"

"That's anger, stupid."

He looked at my face again for a moment, then continued: "Anyway... as I said, I'm afraid we're going to have to do something that's a little more drastic than just killing you."

I decided not to try to convey my feelings about this through facial expressions. At least not until I'd had more practice. I wrote "Disappointment" down on a piece of paper and showed it to him. He crumpled the paper up and dropped it in his wastebasket.

"You see, the problem is, you have uncovered secrets which should have remained buried forever," he continued. "Now we'll have to reverse the damage you have caused. It's fortunate that you got out of the asylum on your own. It saved us the trouble of figuring out a way to get you out without attracting undue attention."

"Secrets? What secrets?"

"Never mind."

"This is where I find out what's going on, right?"

"No."

"Oh." I was disappointed by this, but I tried to be philosophical about it. "Oh well, I guess I'll find out in the end."

"You'd better not."

"That's when I usually find out. Right near the end."

"Not this time, buster."

"Okay. I'll try not to." I wasn't happy about this. I like to find out at the end. "So, if you're not going to kill me, what are you going to do to me?"

"We are going to make it so you never existed—so you were never born."

I thought about this, then slipped him a note with the word "plagiarism" on it. He read the note, then threw it in the wastebasket with my other notes. Then he stood up.

"Let's get this over with."

"All right."

He led me downstairs to a lower level to meet someone he would only refer to as "Clarence".

On the way, we passed rooms full of secret machines the government had been developing. Conklin proudly pointed out a few of them to me.

"That thing that looks like a ray gun is really a new kind of broadcasting. It can shoot a TV show into your head from three hundred yards away."

"That will revolutionize the entertainment industry," I observed.

He nodded. "People won't have to argue about what to watch anymore. Everyone will get to watch his own show."

"Wonderful."

"You'll get the show you want, in the head you want it in."

"I can see that being the slogan for your campaign."

"Yes." He pointed at another gadget. "And that machine over there will make all the evil people in the world six inches tall."

I was interested in this machine. As you know, I'd been looking for ways to make it easier to spot criminals. This might be just the thing.

"Where can I buy one of those gizmos?" I asked, reaching for my wallet.

Conklin shook his head regretfully. "Not on the market yet, I'm afraid. It hasn't even been fully tested. Some of the higher-ups in our government are worried that...well, we just haven't tested it yet, that's all. Good idea though, isn't it?"

I nodded. "It will certainly make my job easier, that's for sure. Say, if the government can do all this, why can't somebody make coffee that tastes good?"

"I don't know. Are you sure you cleaned the pot?"

"Which pot?"

"Maybe the pot needs to be cleaned."

"I still want to know which pot."

He didn't answer. I decided to drop it.

Suddenly another thought occurred to me. "Hey, how are you guys connected with the ghosts?"

"What do you mean?"

"Well... one minute I'm having trouble with ghosts, the next you show up with all this secret government stuff. What's the connection?"

He frowned. "Maybe there is no connection."

I shook my head. "That would be pretty sloppy plotting. The critics would tear us to pieces."

"What critics? There are no critics here." He glanced around to make sure.

"I mean, if this was a detective story, this part wouldn't make much sense."

"It isn't a detective story."

"No, but... oh, never mind. Forget I mentioned it."

I didn't want to tell him I would be writing all this down later. People tend to get stiff and wooden in their actions, with stilted dialogue, when they know it's being recorded for posterity. I didn't want to be stuck with a lot of crap dialogue in my memoirs. The reading public can spot that sometimes. The critics too. And the prize committees. I didn't want to lose the Pulitzer Prize just because of this guy. So I didn't tell him I was going to be writing everything down. As it turned out, Conklin's dialogue was pretty stilted anyway. I figured I'd spiff it up a little bit before I published it, but in the end I didn't bother.

Finally we reached a large room that had one single huge machine in the center of it.

"Meet Clarence," Conklin said proudly.

"Hello, Clarence," I said. I thought maybe I was expected to say more, so I added: "How are you this fine May morning?"

"All right, that's enough talking to the machine," said Conklin. "Impressive, isn't it? Our engineers tell me it uses 3% of the world's oil."

"It's worth it though, I bet."

"Oh yes. The government has been working to perfect a machine like this for many years—since the republic was founded actually. The first unsuccessful prototype was made in 1776 of 'liberty wood', belt buckles, and beaver bottoms, and was powered by Hessians. It failed, of course. The design was too primitive. So another prototype was built. Steam powered this time.

Davy Crockett was sure it would work. But it too failed. And so construction began on yet another model, which ultimately failed as well—they had to rebuild the White House after that one. And so on, down through the years.

"Now, after diverting massive amounts of money from other programs—corn-based coinage, and the vice-president-in-space program, to name but two examples..."

"I usually prefer to have three examples," I pointed out.

"...this facility has finally managed to build a version of the machine that really works. It is a machine that will erase you, Mr. Burly, from existence. Like you were never born. We call it Clarence, after the evil angel in 'It's A Wonderful Life'."

"Hello, Clarence," I said again.

At Conklin's direction, technicians started connecting wires from the machine to my body.

I pointed at something on the machine. "Hey, are those long things teeth?"

"Yes, but don't be alarmed. They're not functional. Strictly part of the design. And that's not real blood dripping off the teeth."

"Good." I heard a low threatening noise coming from the machine. "Is it snarling?"

"I'll turn the volume down."

"Thanks."

The technicians clipped wires onto my eyeballs and asshole.

"This seems kind of dangerous," I said nervously. "Shouldn't we try it out on you first?"

"No, that won't be necessary. It's perfectly safe. Now just relax, take a deep breath, and try not to circulate your blood."

As I took my deep breath, and the final connections were being made between me and the Clarence machine, a white haired exquisitely tailored gentleman smelling of money and votes drifted in looking worried.

"We... uh... lost Kansas," he said.

"There are three government agencies ahead of you," snapped Conklin, as he fiddled with the dials on the machine. "And I have to take care of this man before I do anything else. You'll have to wait over there." He jerked a thumb at a waiting room on the other side of the corridor that was already half-filled with worried looking men.

"Neighboring states are getting curious about the hole," the man persisted.

"I'm busy right now, Senator. Wait over there."

"But..."

"Get over there, buddy," I said. "We're taking care of me first."

He hesitated, then left, wringing his hands fretfully. The nerve of that guy, trying to cut in front of the line like that.

"Now," said Conklin, after he had made a few last minute adjustments, "once I turn on the machine it will read your life history down to the cellular level, then methodically erase it, event by event."

I frowned. "How is that possible? That doesn't seem possible to me."

"It is."

"Maybe you should show me a schematic drawing of the machine and tell me how it works. You could describe the physics involved and we could look over the blueprints while we eat lunch. Then tomorrow, after we've had breakfast, and finished our jogging…"

He shook his head. "There's no time for all that, I'm afraid. I'm already behind schedule. Ready?"

"I guess," I said, in that childish tone I have when I don't get what I want.

He twisted a dial on the machine.

I began seeing my life flashing before my eyes, backwards, with each event slowly fading away, as if it had been exposed to too much sun. There went 2007 down the drain, then 2006. There went my detective career that had never really gotten off the ground. And the three years I spent carrying cement blocks. And my six years of high school. As each memory disappeared I felt my brain growing emptier, more echo-y, and happier. It felt good not having those experiences anymore. Plus, my mind could yodel now.

The procedure was fairly painless, except for all the electricity coursing through me, and all the loud horns blaring in my ears. And I'm not sure what the chisels were digging at me for, but they sure hurt. Maybe that's what they were for.

I felt my fingerprints melt away and my wallet get thinner, as my driver's license and other identity papers disappeared. Finally, I felt my birthmark fade away. The process was complete. I had never been born.

Conklin unhooked me from the machine.

"That didn't hurt, did it?"

"Well, not too much. My rear end is burnt black though. Will that clear up after awhile?"

Conklin frowned and moved off to talk to the technicians who had helped wire me up. "No, I've never heard of it either," said one of them. Then they turned back to me with reassuring smiles. "It will clear up in a couple of weeks," said Conklin.

Despite everything I'd been told about the Clarence machine, and the things I'd seen flashing before my eyes, I didn't really believe I had never been born. I didn't feel any different. And I didn't look any different, except for all the burn marks, the corncob pipe, and the different shirt.

"Your machine's a bust, Conklin," I said, twirling my handlebar mustache. "Nothing has changed."

"Oh no?"

He took me over to the window. We watched 2000 men from a troopship trot by in front of the facility.

"Hey, I thought the men from that troopship were dead!" I said.

"None of the men on that troopship died, because you weren't there to get them killed."

I stared at him in horror. Quickly, I checked to see if the black eyes I usually have were still there. They weren't. My nose wasn't bent in all four directions either. It was like my face had never been punched at all. Then I knew it was true. I had never been born. This was like some kind of Capraesque nightmare!

I was taken down to a lower level and shoved into a cell. Conklin said they couldn't let me go, because I knew too much.

"Oh, come on!" I scoffed. "I don't know anything. Everybody knows that."

"You know about Clarence," Conklin reminded me, "and the machine that makes evil men short, and a number of other things we'd rather not have blabbed all over town at the moment. Or ever. So I hope you'll enjoy your stay with us. It will be a long one."

"Well, I'm sure I will enjoy my stay, enormously, but..."

"The guards will push a piece of meat through your bars once a day."

My cell door clanged shut, and Conklin walked off.

I wondered when the meat was coming. It sounded pretty good.

CHAPTER NINE

I was locked in my cell pretty much 24 hours a day for the next couple of weeks. I complained about that, but they asked me where I would keep a prisoner if I had one, and I had to admit I guessed I'd keep him in a cell. And I'd probably leave him in there most of the time. Just like they were doing to me. So I quit complaining about that. I was off base there. But I felt I was justified in complaining about my rear end. It hadn't cleared up like they had said it would. It just got blacker. And more swollen. I had to sit down the other way. On my face. And that's a very uncomfortable way to sit. You can't see anything except the chair seat. And all you can hear is people laughing. Never go to the government for medical advice, that's what I learned from that experience. Go to a doctor.

There were other prisoners in the cell block, but I didn't socialize with them much. Most of them weren't very interesting to talk to because their minds had been reprogrammed so many times they were just walking error messages. So

I never found out what they were in there for. They probably didn't even know themselves anymore. I did manage to play a few videogames on one of them, but after awhile the guards told me to quit it.

Then one morning my cell block suddenly came alive with frenzied activity: everything was hurriedly scrubbed down and hosed off, including your correspondent; the guards changed into friendlier looking uniforms; and all the prisoners were given party hats. And after a government art director came through, eyed me for a moment, then crossed my legs and put a martini in my hand, I figured something was up. And I was right. The news media was coming.

The facility had always had to deal with occasional visits by newsmen and other busybodies who wanted to know what was going on behind all the barbed wire. Nobody puts boring stuff behind barbed wire, it was felt. Stringing the wire is too much work, for one thing. And there's the expense of buying the wire. "What's the big secret?" people would ask. And, of course, there was no honest way to answer that question without revealing the secret. So the government said nothing.

There were rumors that awful experiments were being conducted in the facility, and that people were being wrongfully imprisoned in there. That was close enough to what was actually going on to make the government very careful about how visitors were dealt with. Refusal to let the news media visit would result in bad publicity, and just lead to more visits, as contradictory as that might seem. Letting them see what was actually going on would be bad too. Since it was all so evil. So they granted them admittance periodically, but only let them see what they wanted them to see.

Everywhere the newsmen went on their carefully guided tours, they saw nothing but nice things: bright airy research centers with handsome scientists looking at test tubes (upside down, but never mind); beautiful atriums where scientists could relax and reflect on all the good they were doing Mankind, and how legal their experiments were; and cheery day care centers where Junior Scientists could romp and play.

Everything looked so nice and innocent, it was a little confusing to the visitors.

"So... why is all this nice activity behind barbed wire and armed guards?" they would ask.

"Let's look over here," the tour guide would say, changing the subject so deftly it was hardly noticeable. And everyone would look over in that new direction, their questions forgotten, at least for the moment.

But the media wasn't always completely taken in by these performances. Sometimes they would catch a glimpse of something evil and smelly behind a door, or a cardboard cutout of a perfectly proportioned scientist would fall over revealing the real hunchback scientist behind it. Sometimes things just didn't feel right. So, despite all the government's efforts, suspicions were aroused.

On this particular Visiting Day, one news

organization, the Central City Cable News Channel, had decided to discover the truth—to, once and for all, get to the bottom of what was going on inside the secret government facility.

While the rest of their news team was taking the tour and obediently asking all the right questions from the list provided, and taking all the right pictures from all the right marks on the floor, and buying all the right items from the gift shop, one member of the team slipped away unseen and made his way down to the lower level of the facility, where I was. This area, when it was shown to visitors at all, was portrayed as a kind of Fun Zone, where scientists and researchers had parties and really let their hair down after a hard day's work. If someone asked about the cells, the answer usually was: "Let's look over here".

I first became aware that an unauthorized and unescorted visitor was snooping around my cell block when my guard got his head bashed in with a microphone, and keys rattled in the lock of my cell door.

"My name's Johnson," the reporter said breathlessly as he struggled with the lock. "I don't know what's been going on in here, but I'm going to find out. Now, once I let you out, remember to..."

At this point he had gotten the door open and I had hit him with a chair, so I didn't get to hear the rest of what he had to say. Grabbing his credentials and his security clearance badge, and outfitting myself with his blazer, oversized capped teeth, and false two foot hair, and putting my party hat on his head so the guards would forever think he was me, I made my escape.

No one paid much attention to me when I joined the other reporters on the tour. With my false hair combed and angled like theirs and a microphone in either hand, I looked just like the rest of them. Even so, I stayed in the back as much as I could, and made it a point to duck behind other reporters whenever a government official looked my way. And I don't think I asked more than five or six questions.

When the tour was concluded, and all of our suspicions had been laid to rest until the next time, we were escorted back to the news bus. As we were walking, one of the newsmen sidled up to me.

"Did you get what we came for?" he asked quietly.

"Huh?"

"Or should we send you back in there?"

"Oh, no, I got what we came for all right. It's... uh... it's in my pocket."

He looked at me strangely for a moment, started to say something, then changed his mind.

I got on the bus with the others, found a seat by a window, then hunched down and hid my face as well as I could. When the bus pulled out, we were waved out of sight by friendly government officials, jolly sentries, and smiling dogs.

For most of the ride back to the news channel's studios, everyone on the bus was turned around in their seats staring at me. Maybe it was the glue dripping down my face from my hair and teeth. Maybe it was my sweaty smile and constant nervous laugh. Or the way I kept saying "Hurry! Hurry!" to the driver. Whatever the reason was, they were staring at me for practically the whole time.

When the bus pulled into the studio parking lot, and I was sure I was safely beyond the reach of the government, I got off the bus and revealed my true identity. Or tried to.

"I'm not really a newsman," I explained to the people around me, as I tugged at my hair and teeth. Apparently I had used a little too much glue when I had put them on. They wouldn't budge.

"Don't say that," one of them said. "TV anchors are kind of newsmen."

"Come on, Johnson," said the man who had spoken to me earlier, taking me firmly by the arm. "You're on in five minutes."

"Yeah, but I'm not really Johnson," I revealed. "I'm some other guy." This sensational piece of news should have stopped him in his tracks, but I guess he didn't completely understand what I was saying. My words were kind of garbled. I wasn't used to talking with such big teeth. "If I could just get these teeth off..." I muttered, yanking at them.

Ignoring my mostly incomprehensible protests, he hustled me into the studio, pushed me down into a chair, then quickly ducked out of sight. Bright lights came on, blinding me. There was thunderous applause. I was on the air!

Looking back on it now, I guess overall I would give my performance a C-. It wasn't really bad, but it definitely had room for improvement.

I couldn't read the teleprompter very well, was one problem. The words were too small and they kept moving all the time. I had to kind of guess at what they said. So that's probably how that war got started. The one that killed so many people. I feel kind of bad about that. My fault, in a way.

I couldn't enunciate very well either. That was another problem with my debut. About the only words people could hear clearly was when I fell backwards off my chair and started cursing a blue streak. They could hear all those words fine.

I never did get to the big expose Johnson was supposed to give at the end of the newscast—the one where all the evil things that were going on inside the government facility would finally be revealed. My reporting was so lackluster during the first half of the show—especially during that teen-oriented segment called Newsdance, which featured the top headlines told to you by dance. I felt silly jiggling around like that—the studio audience grew increasingly restless. Finally they snapped.

"That's not today's weather!" yelled someone in the back. "That's yesterday's sports!"

"He's right!" shouted someone up front.

The situation quickly escalated into a riot. I don't know whose idea it had been to have a studio audience for a news broadcast, or to make this Souvenir Bat Night, but whoever it was had miscalculated.

The audience charged the stage, swinging their bats in all directions, demanding responsible journalism, money, women and dope.

Some of the rioters got up on stage and started horsing around with the equipment, pretending they were broadcasting the news to each other.

"President Buttsmell," announced one young rioter into a microphone, "got a buttache today when he fell on his stupid smell butt. Her-her-her-herherher."

Security guards started moving forward to stop this unauthorized broadcast, but a producer held up his hand and said "Wait."

"Butt butt butt butt smelly butt her-her-her," continued the 'announcer'.

Before I left the studio I saw this 'announcer', and another young man who was making fart sounds with his armpits and buttocks, being signed to fantastic contracts. So I guess you can find talent anywhere. Even show business.

With everyone being distracted by all the rioting, and all the new talent that was being discovered, it seemed like a good opportunity for me to make my escape from the world of journalism. I signed off, then ducked backstage and started looking for a way out.

"Over here, Johnson!" I heard someone shout.

I looked around and saw someone waving to me and holding an emergency exit door open. I knocked him down and ran out, just making it through the door before it closed on me.

I managed to get through all the rioting in the parking lot—they had heard about my broadcast out there too—and got back out onto the street with only minor cuts and bruises, though my fake teeth and hair had sustained major bat damage during the melee. Oh well, they weren't mine anyway.

When I was far enough away from the studio to feel safe, and was sure no one was after me, I stopped and took a look around. It was the first time I'd had a chance to see what Central City looked like now that I had never been born.

It was wonderful.

CHAPTER TEN

For the rest of the afternoon I wandered around Central City with a big smile on my face. What an improvement! Everything was better now that I wasn't born.

People were happier, buildings were taller and straighter, the sky was bluer, dogs barked better and louder. There weren't as many graveyards, or broken noses, and there were far fewer fires. People were right about me being a troublemaker. I saw that now. We probably should have done something about me a long time ago.

After awhile my smile started to fade a bit and I began feeling a little insulted by how much better everything was now. It was getting ridiculous. I mean, how come the pavement was better? What did I have to do with that? Come on! But I couldn't stay angry for long. Things were just too great.

All my personal problems had gone away too. No debts to be paid, no lifelong enemies to battle, no relatives coming to visit and eat all my food, and, above all, no problems with the authorities. Conklin and his government thugs didn't even know I had escaped yet. And they never would as long as that party hat stayed on Johnson's head. And I didn't have to worry about the local police or the people from the loony bin looking for me either. There was nobody to look for. I didn't exist. They had never heard of me. I proved this to myself by boldly confronting a policeman on a street corner.

"Are you looking for me?" I asked.
"Who are you?"
"Nobody."
"Then no."
"You don't want to arrest me?"
He hesitated before answering. "I didn't a minute ago."
"That's all I wanted to know. So long, sucker."
"So long."

He watched me go, suspiciously. I still looked suspicious, of course. You can't change your looks. That shifty expression most of us have will always be there whether we've been born or not. But they can't arrest us for it.

A few people on the streets did recognize me, but it wasn't as Frank Burly. They recognized me from my television appearance as the reporter Johnson. They waved at me when they saw me and said something about me being lousy. I waved back. I offered to sign autographs for them, but they said maybe later. Fame sure is fleeting. I forget who originally said that.

Since I wasn't born, I expected my house and office to have other people occupying them, but when I checked them out I found they were both empty. It looked like no one had been in them since they were built. I guess I was the only person on Earth willing to inhabit them. That was a break for me. My lack of taste saved me some trouble there. I moved right back in.

My house was broken down and filled with cobwebs, but not as many as there had been before. It looked quite a bit nicer, in fact. So everything was fine on that score.

But I soon found there were problems associated with not being born. No birthday presents, was the first thing I noticed. When September 22nd rolled around, nobody thought it was an important day at all. I looked in my mailbox a couple of times, but there was nothing there.

A much bigger problem for me though, was my sudden total lack of documentation.

My driver's license was no longer valid. Gotta be born to have one of those. At least that's what they told me down at the DMV (after four hours!). I had no bank account either. No private investigator's license. And my library card was no good.

"Well, shit," I said.

"Shh!" they replied.

I couldn't even prove I was old enough to drink, so I found myself in the embarrassing position of having to ask kids to buy beer for me. They did it, but some of them were crying the whole time.

The worst part of it was that I knew there was no way for me to correct any of this. It's always possible, no matter how bad things get, no matter how much you've screwed up your life and smeared your own reputation, to start a new life for yourself somewhere else. Idaho, maybe. They don't know about us in Idaho. But you have to be alive first. And be able to prove it. Otherwise you're up Shit Crick. I'd been up Shit Crick before, of course, lots of times—I ran for Mayor in '96—but I'd never liked it there. So I wasn't happy about being there again.

But you can't just sit around complaining all the time, just because things aren't going your way. There's no money in that, kids. At some point you have to get hold of yourself and start striving to do something positive with your life. The only positive thing I could think of to do right then was to get revenge on the little pricks who had gotten me into this. So I began positively looking for Ed and Fred.

I tried all their usual haunts first; the bars and coffee shops they frequented; the newspaper boxes they favored; and that haunted house at the carnival they enjoyed heckling. They weren't in any of their usual places. I decided I needed to expand my search.

I went to an area on the Near North Side called Odd Town. That's where you'll find all the people who are a little too odd to live anywhere else. Some zoning thing, I guess. There are lots of aged Hippies in Odd Town, as well as Lazies, Yellers, Stealies and Stupids. I figured even if the ghosts weren't there, these people might know where I should look. I thought they might be a little more on the ghosts' wavelength than, say, the guys in the Financial District. As it turned out, I was right.

I talked to a number of unusual people on the streets of Odd Town, many of whom were convinced of some very surprising things: that capitalism would soon be gone and be replaced by something else—photography, I think they said; that the world is being secretly run by politicians; that school teachers are trying to control our minds with their textbooks; that the dinosaurs evolved into flying saucers; all sorts of weird ideas like that. Unfortunately, none of them knew anything about my two ghosts. They just knew everything else.

I spent nearly an hour with one man in a bar who introduced me to what he said was a six foot tall invisible rabbit. I thought he was nuts and told him so, in that nice way I have. He wasn't offended by my skepticism. He seemed to think that mine was an interesting take on the situation—an alternative view—and was glad we were all taking part in the conversation. Then he told me about how little actual work he did, and how much he enjoyed wasting everybody else's time. He said he didn't know where my ghosts might be, but if they did turn up he suggested they might want to play basketball with his rabbit. After he had gone, the bartender told me I was right. The guy was nuts.

"Isn't there a rabbit?" I asked.

"There's a rabbit, sure," he said, "but he left three hours ago."

He also said I should watch out for the guy because he had just killed a couple of high school kids.

Then someone I ran into on the streets—an old man who said he needed money, but could no longer remember why or how much—told me about a society nearby where they kept track of rains of frogs and rivers of blood and supernatural stuff like that. They might have some info on my ghosts. I gave the man a dime for this information, which he said wasn't nearly enough, and headed for the building he had pointed out to me.

The society was called The Central City Center For Psychic And Paranormal Research, or TCCCFPAPR for short. It was a beehive of activity when I arrived, with researchers running around clutching stories hot off the newswire with wild looks in their eyes.

"Ghost train on the West Side!" yelled one.

"You mean the train has ghosts in it, or the train itself is a ghost?" he was asked.

"What difference does it make?"

"Well, there's a world of difference, Bob..."

"We'll discuss it later. Just get somebody over there!"

"A river of blood just appeared next to the regular river of blood!" broke in another researcher excitedly.

"Two rivers of blood!" said the man next to him, slapping his forehead.

"Somebody just dropped a house on the President!" said someone else.

I corralled one of them as he went scurrying by and told him I was looking for two ghosts. He looked at me like I was a hick.

"What kind of cornball thing is that to be looking for?"

"Well, I dunno."

He told me they didn't have time for old-fashioned ghosts like mine. This was the most paranormal activity they'd ever monitored. Strange phenomena of all kinds were occurring everywhere—weird manifestations that made my ghosts seem corny by comparison.

"Like what?"

He thought for a moment. "Well, last week the whole city was briefly under miles of ocean."

"I must have been in the can when that happened."

"And then the city was hit by a bunch of comets. And there was a World War there for a minute. And the spitball was legalized briefly, so we could all throw spitballs again without fear of being suspended. And there was that big Titanic race in the harbor—a race that the experts had said could never happen. And…"

"Gee, I sure must go to the can a lot." A thought occurred to me. "Hey, maybe the government is doing all this. Did you ever think of that?"

He sneered at this idea. "Governments don't do anything. That's just something people say when they don't know what's going on and want to sound like they do."

"Well, yeah," I admitted, "I do say that when I don't know what's going on, but in this case…"

"Get out of here."

I said I wasn't leaving until I got some kind of clue, something to go on. This is where being big and slow to be satisfied comes in handy. After a moment's vain struggle to release himself from my dull, uncomprehending grip, he said I might try The Very Haunted House. I asked what that might be.

"We haven't had time to look into it," he said, "but we've been getting a lot of reports from a neighborhood a few blocks south of here. Apparently some house is so full of ghosts they're spilling out into the street. The neighbors have been complaining about it."

I thanked him, and left. Finally I had a lead!

When I got to the neighborhood he had told me about, I wished I'd remembered to get the exact address. All the houses on both sides of the street looked pretty rundown. They all looked like they could be haunted. I was trying to figure out which one to try first, when I saw a ghost suddenly appear three feet above the street, fall to the ground, sit up, looking confused, then run off.

I followed him.

CHAPTER ELEVEN

I followed the ghost to an old apparently abandoned Victorian home, and watched as he walked up to the door, knocked, listened for a moment, then dissolved through the door into the house.

I went up the steps and knocked on the door. I heard a faint eerie "come in", but nobody came to open the door. I tried the knob. The door was locked. I tried shouldering my way in, but only succeeded in hurting my shoulder.

I knocked again, but all I got for my efforts were a couple of more "come ins", a "wipe your feet", and another sore shoulder.

I tried to waft through the door like I had seen the ghost do. You never know. But all I got out of that experiment was a chipped tooth.

I took a walk around the house to see if I could find an open window. At first I couldn't find one, but after awhile, when I was sure no one was looking, I found one. I climbed through.

There didn't seem to be anyone in the place. It was, to all appearances, just an old empty house. The furniture was covered with layers of dust. The mirrors were streaked with grime. Rocking chairs were rocking by themselves. The fireplace was going on and off. Just an old empty house.

Then I heard a noise. A strange wailing sound. It didn't sound human. Then I heard footsteps on the stair. They didn't sound human either. But when I looked at the staircase (not human), there was nobody there! Then the wailing sound came again. It sounded like it was coming from one of the closets, so I opened the door. There were thousands of ghosts in there. They tumbled out and began swarming all around me, shrieking and wailing, and laughing unearthly laughs.

Normally I would have been scared shitless, because, like I said before, dead things that don't act dead scare me. But I'd seen so much of this kind of thing lately, it just didn't make much of an impression on me anymore.

"Have any of you seen a ghost named Ed Brannigan? Or Fred C. Cramer? Either one. I'm looking for them. That's Brannigan. B-r-a-double-n-i-g-a-n."

The ghosts shrieked louder and wailed even more hideously, but none of them volunteered any information. I pushed through them and checked to see if maybe Ed and Fred were in the closet someplace. Maybe behind that stack of old ghosts in the corner. They weren't.

When I straightened back up and stood there for a minute, scratching my head, I noticed the ghosts had stopped wailing and were floating in the center of the room, staring at me and looking confused and vaguely pissed.

I pushed through them to the kitchen and looked around there. They followed. One tried a "boo!" but it didn't get any response from me, so he didn't try it again.

I came back out to the living room, after finding nothing in the kitchen, and looked in the closet again. The ghosts watched me, plainly not sure what the deal was with me. I was supposed to be afraid of them. But I wasn't. They didn't get it.

I asked them again about Ed Brannigan, and finally, after they had wailed some more, and I had started giving them the correct spelling of the name again, one of them answered me.

"He and Fred aren't here. They've been gone for almost a week."

"Do you know where they've gone?"

"No."

"Well, crap."

I sat down on a chair full of ghosts. They scattered, grousing. I didn't bother to apologize. I was pissed. Ed and Fred used to be here. But "used to" only counts in horseshoes. I had to find out where they were now. This place was just another dead end.

Now that the ghosts were convinced that there was no point in trying to scare me, they went about their business. Which, I noticed, involved trying to get comfortable in a severely overcrowded environment; with too many ghosts crowded into each chair; ghosts stacked up on the tops of bookcases; ghosts neatly folded up in drawers; even ghosts coming out of faucets. This house had a lot of ghosts in it. I started to get curious about that.

"Hey, how come there are so many of you?"

"We don't know," said one of the ghosts standing on my head.

"We don't know," said a ghost in the cuckoo clock. "We don't know. We don't know."

"I know," said a ghost named Nugent.

I looked at him. None of the ghosts there were particularly happy, but Nugent was easily the glummest ghost in the place. He said that government interference had caused the increased ghost population. I asked him how he knew that, pointing out that I'd heard only stupid people who didn't know what they were talking about blamed the government for things, and he said he used to work for the government, that's how he knew. Worked for them for years. Then one day, right in the middle of a top secret experiment, just after he had said "That ought to do it", he suddenly found himself here, dead. Some of his co-workers were here too. I tried to pump him for more information—what was the nature of this top secret experiment he spoke of, let's take a look at the blueprints, and where the hell were Ed and Fred?—but he didn't want to talk anymore. He just sat there sulking.

"I'm tired of talking to you, Nugent," I said finally.

"Ditto."

I got up to go. This had been a wasted trip. Just like all of the trips I had ever taken in my life. What's it all about, anyway? Would somebody please tell me that? Just then, on that philosophical note, the front door opened and Ed and Fred breezed in.

"Hi everybody," said Fred, cheerfully.

"What's the score, fellas?" asked Ed, rhetorically, as they both bounded up the stairs.

I stared at them. It was Ed and Fred, all right, but there was something different about them. All the ghosts were staring at them too. Then I realized what it was—what was different. Ed and Fred weren't ghosts anymore! They were real men! I suddenly felt like I was in the middle of some kind of a Pinocchio picture.

The other ghosts were stunned. They didn't know what to make of it. But I figured out what had happened quick enough. Ed and Fred had never hired me now, because I didn't exist, so they had never had an opportunity to be killed by me. That didn't explain why the other ghosts knew them so well. Or why they seemed to have a room upstairs here. But you can't understand everything. At least, I can't.

I bounded up the stairs after them.

When I found them they were in their room packing up their stuff into two big suitcases to move to their cool bachelor pad they'd just rented downtown. They had dates tonight, they said, with a couple of dames who had bones that just wouldn't quit.

I confronted them angrily. "Look what you bastards did to me," I said, pointing at myself. "I don't exist anymore. I was never born. My library card's not valid." I took the card out of my wallet and held it up to them so they could see.

"It's not our fault," said Ed. "How could it be? We've never even met you now."

"That's right," said Fred. "We couldn't have caused you any trouble, because there ain't no you!"

I was getting steamed. "If you confuse me one more time, I'm gonna..."

"You're gonna what?" jeered Ed. "What are you gonna do?"

I landed a haymaker on Ed's chin, then drove a left jab into Fred's new solar plexus. They both went over backwards, squawking.

"Hey, Rube!" yelled Fred.

As I jumped on them and began knocking their teeth loose, the other ghosts joined in the fight—kicking me, biting me, and, by combining their forces and using all the ectoplasm they had, lifting up heavy objects and braining me with them.

I had Ed and Fred down and was punching them for all I was worth, but I had been hit so many times I was starting to get a little woozy. The third time the ghosts brought the dresser down on my head, I finally collapsed to the floor on top of the unconscious forms of Ed and Fred.

The ghosts all piled on top of us, banging away at my head with everything they had. Finally, after I hadn't moved or said "ouch" for several minutes, they stopped hitting me and backed away. Then one of the ghosts shrieked in terror.

Three new ghosts were rising up from the bodies on the floor: Ed, Fred, and me.

CHAPTER TWELVE

"You killed us again, you bastard!" howled Ed. "And I just bought a full length mirror!" complained Fred.

"Never mind that, you little pricks, look what you did to me!" I pointed a transparent finger at my twisted corpse. "I'm dead too!"

"Good!" said Fred.

"We're glad!" said Ed.

We all swung our fists at the same time, the force of the blows blowing us all apart. We spent the next ten minutes retrieving our body parts from under the furniture and yelling abuse at each other, with my mouth under the couch having a shouting match with Ed's face in the fireplace, while our hands and arms looked for us.

Once I had put myself back together again, and got my eyes into the right holes, I saw that Ed and Fred, and some of the younger ghosts, were over in the corner of the room kicking my corpse and calling it a fat son of a bitch. That really made me mad. I'm not fat. I've just got fat bones.

The first fight I'd had with the inhabitants of The Very Haunted House had been frustrating. Round Two was a pleasure. I was finally able to lay a glove on the bastards. We were on equal terms now, substance-wise. And I had the advantage of being bigger and angrier than any of them. So it was no contest. I beat the stuffings out of them. I was literally mopping the floor with them. Beating the rugs too. And ringing the doorbell. I tried painting the walls with them, but the paint wouldn't stay on their wispy little heads, no matter how far I dunked them into the can.

The battle didn't last as long as I wanted it to. Nothing really worthwhile ever does, the philosophers tell us. And they are right, as usual. The ghosts weren't enjoying the fight as much as I was, so after fifteen or twenty minutes, most of them split. I'm not sure where they went, but I did hear screams of "Oh no, not again!" from one of the neighboring houses. So that's probably where they went. That's where I'd start looking.

I worked off my remaining excess energy and anger by trashing the place. That is, I tried to trash it. Unfortunately, I hadn't had much experience at being a ghost yet. I couldn't materialize enough to get a good grip on anything valuable. My ectoplasm kept fading on me. Then I'd have to start all over again. I managed to tip over a small odd-shaped table after twenty minutes of sustained effort, but it wasn't the kind of wholesale destruction I had been hoping to cause. And it turned out that the odd-shaped table had actually been tipped over already and I had spent the twenty minutes getting it right-side-up again. At that point I figured the hell with it.

I went back upstairs to take a look at my body. It was in pretty bad shape. Dents everywhere, limbs pointing in all the wrong directions, the odd tooth gone, and footprints all over it. It was a mess. I wasn't sure what I was supposed to do with it, but I was pretty sure I shouldn't just leave it where it was.

The problem was, I didn't know how to move it. My hands just went right through it when I tried to pick it up. I knew it was possible to move it, because I had seen Ed and Fred move solid objects around with relative ease. But darned if I could figure out how they did it.

I tried sliding into my body and operating it from the inside. That didn't work. I didn't think it would, but it was worth a try. I wouldn't recommend other people trying it though. It's pretty nasty in there. Dark, claustrophobic, damp and smelly. And I think I heard rats in there. I got back out of there pretty quick.

After experimenting for awhile, I found that by clenching every muscle in my ghostly body—sort of gritting myself—I could materialize enough to be able to move things around. The more I practiced, the better I got at this.

Finally I decided I was ready. I picked up my corpse's legs and began dragging it slowly out of the room. I hit the head on a few things, but I decided that that probably didn't matter at this point. I didn't know whether I would ever be using that head again or not, but I certainly wasn't using it now.

I dragged my body down the two flights of stairs to the living room, my head thumping on each step, then dragged it out of the house, across the yard, and onto the sidewalk, as the few remaining ghosts in the house watched me from the window, occasionally rubbing the knots on their heads. They didn't try to stop me or get me to come back. They'd had enough of me. They probably wished I had left sooner.

Now that the battle was over, and I had successfully retrieved my personal property, I took a moment to review my situation. It didn't look good. I was in a pretty tough spot. Not only was I never born, now I was dead too. Things hadn't been going too well for me lately. I decided the first thing I should do was seek medical help. My body was looking worse by the minute. One of my ears was about to fall off. It had never been this loose. I needed to see a doctor right away.

I spent the next three hours laboriously dragging my corpse down the street towards the hospital—with people screaming and running away, policemen anxiously blowing their whistles at me, and dogs trying their damnedest to pull my corpse in the opposite direction from where I wanted it to go. It was a pain in the butt. And I mean that in both the literal and the philosophical sense.

After awhile I noticed I was scraping my body's eyebrows off on the pavement. I didn't care. I never knew what eyebrows were for anyway. Artists have since told me that you need them so you can move them around to express your feelings. Surprise, or anger, or mounting fear. Useful expressions like that. I've always kept them in the same place on my face. Maybe that's been my problem all along. Maybe that's why I got passed over for promotion so many times, and why I never made it in Society, and why I got arrested and ambushed so often. Maybe I should have been using my eyebrows more. Anyway, I scraped 'em off.

By late that afternoon I was sitting in the hospital waiting room, reading a magazine, with my body in the chair next to me, surrounded by every fly that had ever lived.

A terrified nurse finally ushered me in to the doctor's office. I dragged my body in and got it up on the examination table, while the doctor watched from the top of a filing cabinet. When I finally convinced him that I wouldn't be leaving until he had examined the body, and if he didn't hurry up, I would start bringing it up to where he was, he reluctantly climbed down and began to check it over.

It was a difficult examination for a number of reasons. There was no pulse to check, no breathing to listen to, no reflexes to measure, no eyebrows to indicate my current mood, nothing. But probably the biggest problem was communication.

"Cough."

I coughed.

"Not you. Your body."

"Look," I said, "this is getting confusing. For the past hour…"

"Just cough… not you."

When he had finished the examination, he told me I could get dressed. I told him I was already dressed. He said he meant my body. There was that communication problem again. I suggested that the next time we do this he should point to which one of me he's talking to. The dead one or the other dead one. He said there wouldn't be a next time. I said never mind then.

He wrote the results of my tests down on my chart. I watched him do this, worriedly.

"How long do I have, Doc?"

"Until what?"

"Just answer the question."

"You don't have any time. You're dead."

"I know, but, now what? I mean, what pills should I take? And how often? What's your professional advice?"

He advised me to put my body under six feet of dirt and leave it there until Christ came back. He said that was the best thing I could do for it now. If I insisted on giving it something, he suggested flowers.

It wasn't the advice I'd hoped for, and I wished he had given me some pills to take, but he was the doctor. I nodded glumly and started dragging my body back towards the elevators. Flowers. I would remember that.

CHAPTER THIRTEEN

I'm not the kind of guy who gives up easily. I don't do anything easily. I've always done things the hard way. It's my style, darnit.

So I didn't take the doctor's advice right away. Six feet under ground might be the best place for my body, but I could always put it there. There was no rush. The ground wasn't going anyplace. And the longer I kept my body above ground, the better chance there was of a better option coming along. Maybe some new medicine. Or maybe I'd develop a style that wasn't so pointless.

I dragged my body back to my house and tried to get on with my life, such as it was. I tried to make the best of a bad situation. I'm like that. Upbeat, that's me.

I wasn't sure where I should keep my body at first. It didn't seem right to just stuff it in a closet—it didn't seem respectful. And besides, the closet was pretty full already. With better stuff. There was no way I was going to take my tool box out of there. That tool box was brand new.

By bending it a little, I found I could get my

body into the closet without taking anything else out, but every time I tried to close the door there would be a neck sticking out. That wasn't acceptable to me. It didn't look tidy enough. Besides, there was no way to lock it now, and I had that new tool box in there.

Finally I gave up on the idea of trying to store it somewhere out of sight, and just started treating it more or less like a house guest.

I propped it up in a chair, put slippers on its feet, and turned on a reading lamp, in case it suddenly was able to read. I tried to feed it—it looked kind of hungry to me—but the food just stayed in its mouth, or nose, wherever I put it. It didn't go anyplace after that, which is what you want.

After a few days I was putting on TV shows I thought my corpse would like, taking it to boxing matches, and trying to play tennis with it. That whole game was a farce. I couldn't hit the ball and my body couldn't hit it back. We just stood there.

My ghostly body wasn't much more use to me than my regular body was. Due to my lack of substance, it was hard for me to do even the simplest of domestic tasks. Cooking was difficult, cleaning and dusting were more trouble than they were worth, and trying to rotate the tires on my car was a complete waste of time. I managed to get one tire off, but not the others. And then I couldn't get the first tire back on again. Same thing happened when I tried to re-shingle my roof, and rotate the paint on my house. I've got to remember not to start projects I can't finish. That's a good lesson for all of us to remember.

As if I didn't have enough problems, I started getting complaints from my neighbors. They said strange noises were coming out of my house at night. Hey, can I help it if I fall over things? And talk to myself through a bullhorn? Is that my fault? They said there seemed to be a spirit haunting the place, which apparently violated some kind of neighborhood covenant. They were worried I might owe them some money.

Finally a neighborhood committee showed up at my house to discuss these issues with me. I was happy to have this discussion with them, because I was getting a little bored with my own company. It would be nice, I felt, to talk to someone new. Someone whose mouth moved.

Unfortunately, the meeting didn't go very well. My neighbors seemed extremely uncomfortable all the time they were in my home. For one thing, there seemed to be two of me there. One transparent and the other dead. I said there was actually only one of us—I was a ventriloquist. They asked which one of me was the ventriloquist. I wasn't ready for that question, didn't know what to say, so after awhile I just chased them around with a poker until they left. After that, there were no more complaints. But no more visitors either.

Then one evening while I was playing checkers with my body (three hours and no moves yet!) I decided I couldn't continue to live this way. Something had to be done. I had to try to find a way to bring my body back to life, or this checker game would never end.

Since doctors hadn't been able to help me, I tried taking my body to a repair shop. The sign in the window of the shop said: 'We fix anything" with a long string of reassuring asterisks. I figured a shop with that much confidence in itself was the place for me. I materialized myself as well as I could—and I was getting better at this. You could still see through me, but not for as many miles—and dragged my body down to the shop.

I told Sid, the repairman, my problem. He looked my body over for awhile, then shook his head. "I don't like the look of that head."

"You don't? Wait a minute. I'll make it smile."

He shook his head again. "I'm pretty sure you're going to need a new head."

"No, I want to keep the head, if I can."

He looked at me the way all repairmen look at me when I say something like that, then did some figuring. "Cost you five hundred dollars," he said finally. "Come back this afternoon. I'll have it fixed up as good as new." Then he made some rapid tiny sounds with his mouth that I later figured out were asterisks.

When I came back that afternoon, Sid had gotten my body looking pretty good. I especially liked the huge biceps (compressed air did the trick there, he revealed), and the nice healthy color he had painted my face, but my body still didn't work, which was mainly what I was looking for. It just laid there on the hydraulic lift, leaking oil.

I told Sid I didn't want my body to just look good, which it did, I wanted it to be able to earn a living, with me inside it. He said if I wanted that I would have to pop for a new head. I said I wouldn't, that I thought the current head was good enough, that it still had some wear left in it, and reminded him that the customer was always right. He said that usually wasn't the case in his experience. He couldn't remember the last time a customer was right. I said I was thinking seriously of taking my valuable business somewhere else, and he said he was glad to hear that. So that's where we left it.

We argued about the bill for awhile, an argument which I finally won by just disappearing. Sid put my body in a storage area with a bunch of other crap that hadn't been paid for, but I just dragged it away that night. Score one for me.

Feeling I needed help of a more supernatural nature than Sid, I took my body to Odd Town. I had seen a number of occult-type characters hanging around there the last time I was in the area—exorcists, sorcerers, you name it—all anxious to make a quick Earthly buck. You'd think people with magical powers wouldn't have to work for a living in the crappiest part of town, but you would be wrong. I've seen them there.

I went to the first sorcerer I could find, and told him what I wanted. He looked at my body doubtfully.

"I don't..." he began.

"I want to keep the head," I snapped.

He shrugged, said the customer was always right (ha!), and went to work.

After fiddling with my body for awhile, and

chanting gibberish over it, including what sounded like garbled lyrics to several popular songs such as Pennsylvania 6-5000, and sprinkling what looked like, and turned out to be, barbeque sauce over it, he announced grandly that my body had been successfully brought back to life. Then he kicked it a little to make it move briefly. He didn't get paid either. As I dragged my body back out onto the street again, he shouted at me that he'd turn me into a newt if I didn't pay. I said I bet he wouldn't.

I tried several other sorcerers on the same block, but it turned out the first guy I had gone to was the best one. They were surprised I had gotten in to see him.

As I said earlier, I don't give up easily. But I do give up eventually. And the time had come to admit to myself that the doctors and the fix-it shop men were probably right. I was dead. And I wasn't coming back. I would have to continue to walk the Earth as a ghost until a place opened up for me in Heaven.

That was one good thing I had gotten out of all of this. At least I knew how the afterlife worked now. I even knew how long I had to wait. One of the ghosts in The Very Haunted House had tipped me off that I was due to check in to Heaven in 2018. He said we were going to be sharing the same cloud—46B Upper Level, Next To The Fire Door—when it became available.

I don't know where he got all his information, but he said my death was supposed to occur in Germany in the summer of 2018, when I was destined to blunder into the middle of a nuclear standoff between the superpowers and fart. So until that year rolled around, it looked like there was nothing else for me to do but wait.

CHAPTER FOURTEEN

There's something about being a ghost that makes you want to laugh. A big graveyard laugh. You're dead, and that's funny. The sun's out but you're not getting any warmth from it. And there's something funny about that too. Everything's funny. Ha ha hoo hoo hrrrrr! But deep down you know it's not really a laughing matter. It's serious. So serious, you can't help but laugh. Ha ha hooey hrrrr!

Since I didn't have any immediate use for my body, and I still didn't feel comfortable with the idea of burying it, I put it in storage. No point in dragging it everywhere I went. I thought I had to, at first, but a couple of times I didn't and nobody said anything, so I figured it must be optional. Just as well. The pants and hair were being scraped off by the cement sidewalks. It's bad enough being dead, you don't want to be bald and have your butt hanging out too. Besides, I couldn't be dragging a lot of dead weight around all the time. I had work to do.

You'd think that once you're dead that should

put an end to your obligations. That's the way most people figure it. Whatever the afterlife holds for them, they're confident they can kick back and relax at that point and let somebody else do the work. But it's not so. Ghosts are expected to do all kinds of things.

You're supposed to hang around places you frequented in life, for example. So I went to those places and hung around. Stories of haunted strip clubs, drunk tanks, and unemployment lines followed me around town wherever I went.

And once you get to these places, you can't just stand around picking your nose until it's time to go home. No, that would be too easy. Ghosts are expected to trudge up and down stairs, move things around in mysterious and spooky ways, and float from room to room saying all kinds of scary things like "boo" and "get back". It's a lot of work, let me tell you. A lot of nights I just went through the motions, or put in a token appearance. In my more reflective moments I wondered what it was all about.

It probably wouldn't have been so bad if I wasn't so clumsy. I don't know how a ghost can fall down stairs, but I did it. And I don't know why it hurt, but it did. And just about every time I tried to rattle some pots and pans to scare somebody, I'd end up with the whole kitchen on top of me. So instead of all the spooky rattling, my victim would just hear an explosion of sound followed by a lot of unearthly cursing. It was probably scarier the way I did it, but that didn't make me like it any better.

As a ghost, you're supposed to make it a point to haunt the people you knew when you were alive, so I appeared all over my neighborhood, giving old acquaintances a scare.

"In life I was your gasoline customer, Frank Burly," I would wail.

"So what?"

"I don't know."

"You want some gas?"

"Not really," I would say, rattling some chains.

"Well piss off then."

"Righty-o."

That sort of thing. Kind of pointless, really. I mean, what exactly is it supposed to accomplish? The gas station guy didn't get what it was about any more than I did.

Aside from all the work I had to do, there were other things that annoyed me about being a ghost. It's hard to stay in one place, for instance. You're too insubstantial, that's the scientific explanation for it. You don't weigh enough.

You'll be scaring some dame, for example, saying "boo!" and "look out for me!" and "I'm trouble!" and so on, snappy horror picture dialogue like that, and a gust of wind will pick you up and the next thing you know you're wrapped around the city limits sign five miles away, or stuck to the bottom of somebody's shoe, heading off in the wrong direction. And the dame you were scaring is long gone. You can forget about her. You won't be scaring her anymore today.

Another problem is you can't eat anything.

Well, you can, but it's not very satisfying. All the food you eat just falls out through the back of your neck onto the floor. The only good thing about that is you get to eat it again. So you only need one French fry to have French fries all day. It's easy on the budget, but, like I said, it's unsatisfying.

But what really got my goat about the whole ghost business, was that after doing all that work I had to do, people didn't even believe I had been doing it. They thought everything I had done could be explained away. They said I was just some kind of natural phenomenon: an air pressure change, imperfections in a window, lights from a passing car, a hallucination, or, most insulting of all, bits of undigested beef.

"I don't believe in ghosts," people would tell me, with a smirk, when I showed up.

This statement would always make me mad.

"Who cares whether you believe in ghosts or not? Shut up!"

"I think you're bits of beef."

"Well I'm not!"

"That's my theory."

"It's wrong!"

"Ha!"

According to one local newspaper only 32% of the population of Central City believed in "The Arguing Ghost", as they had begun to call me. The rest said I was bullshit.

A few enterprising people tried to take my picture for the tabloid magazines, and I kept trying to pose for those pictures. We could both make some money if we could get a good picture. We could split it. But we never managed to come up with anything convincing. The pictures all looked faked, especially the one of me shaking hands with Eisenhower. That one really was faked. I'm not sure why we did that. Only 14% of the people believed in me after that picture came out. After awhile, even I started to think I was bullshit.

But probably the worst part of the whole experience was the boredom. Halloween was a busy time for me, of course, but once November rolled around things started to really slow down. Not much call for ghosts on Thanksgiving. People want turkeys then.

At one point I got so bored I started feeling a little sorry for myself. That felt good. That cheered me up. So I tried feeling sorry for other people to see if that would feel just as good. It didn't. I went back to me. Poor Burly, I thought. Poor old Frankie. What a raw deal he got. He deserved so much better.

Then one evening while I was feeling sorry for myself over my French fry dinner, a special report came on TV. It was that long overdue expose of the secret government facility that I had been asked to deliver months before.

The reporter whose place I had taken, Johnson, had finally been released by the government after his hair and capped teeth grew back and they realized they were holding the wrong man.

Johnson was brought on with great fanfare ("And now, here he is... her-her-herherher... Stan

Johnson!") and everyone waited expectantly for him to tell all about the government facility, and all the evil secrets he'd uncovered there. But his mind had apparently been wiped clean before his release, and all he could remember now was how to flip his lips with his finger. After a few minutes of this, another reporter came on and flipped his lips the other way, to make sure we got a balanced report. So the long anticipated story was a bust. Of course, that is show business for you. They can't all be gems.

But the show wasn't a total loss. It had given me an idea. I would take my body back to the government facility and hook it up to the Clarence machine again. If the machine could fix it so I had never been born, I reasoned shrewdly, maybe it could fix it so I had never been killed. You never know. There were plenty of dials on that machine. Maybe one of them could reverse all of this.

I ate my dinner a couple more times to fortify myself, then went to get my body out of storage.

CHAPTER FIFTEEN

It took quite awhile to get to the government facility. My body hadn't gotten any lighter while it was in storage. In fact, it actually seemed a little heavier to me. I thought maybe it had been eating something in there somehow, but the extra weight just turned out to be some kids riding on it. I scared them off. Darn kids.

On the way down the street, people who had seen my body around a lot waved at it. I made it wave back.

I knew from my previous visit that the facility was well guarded, so gaining access wouldn't be easy. I would have to be tricky.

Accordingly, I presented my body at the main gate as an employee who was ready to start his eight hour shift. I balanced lunchboxes on my body as props. Unfortunately, my body didn't have the proper security badge, nor did it know the day's password, though, with my invisible help, it made over 150 wild guesses before the guards said it couldn't have any more. 150 was the limit. We were turned away.

Then I tried passing off my body as a visiting 4-star general, here to inspect the facility. The problems here were: this wasn't a military facility, I still had no security badge, my body wasn't wearing a uniform of any kind, and the guards remembered me from before.

Then I decided maybe I was trying to be too tricky. My experience with the government is there's always somebody who isn't doing his job. Maybe I should just look for the gate that that guy was guarding.

I found it on the west side of the facility, near the back. The guard was snoring away like a steam engine next to an open gate. Teenagers were running out of the facility past him carrying cases of government liquor and saying "Yes!" I edged past him and was in.

But I wasn't home free. There were guards on the inside of the facility too. Thousands of them. And they wouldn't all be asleep.

My ghostly self could get past any guard easily enough, of course. It was the slowly dragged corpse I had with me that was hard to get past the guards unseen. It took me an hour to negotiate one turn in the hallway. My right eye kept getting caught on one of the corners. I started to hate that eye.

All that afternoon, each guard in turn would watch, with narrowing eyes, the corpse that was slowly coming towards him, and listen, with narrowing ears, to the unearthly grunts that were coming from something invisible nearby. When my corpse finally got close enough to the guard for him to be able to challenge it without leaving his post, he would order it to halt. It would halt. The guard would then approach the corpse and prod it with his bayonet, demanding to see its security pass. After he got no response he would then invariably bend over my body for a closer look. That's when he'd get the fire extinguisher in the head. Then it was on to the next guard in the next corridor.

In this way I worked my way deeper into the facility towards the Clarence machine.

On the way, I passed by a number of storage rooms, which were packed to the rafters with secret new gadgets the government had been developing. I looked into each of these rooms briefly, partially out of curiosity, partially because that's the way my face was pointing anyway, but mostly because I couldn't remember exactly where the Clarence room was.

Finally, after I had dragged my corpse nearly half a mile through countless corridors, and up and down hundreds of concrete steps, and worn out three fire extinguishers on the guards, I got to the heavy iron door I remembered from before. Behind this door was the Clarence machine. I expected to have trouble getting in, but the door was unlocked this time. And a quick check confirmed that no one was inside. That was a relief. That meant I could do what I came to do with no interruptions. I started dragging my corpse into the room.

All machines have their little idiosyncrasies, but they all have one thing in common—they have to be turned on. Getting Clarence turned on took me nearly an hour, during which time I broke several dials, accidentally unscrewed one of the legs, and spilled mustard on the motor. But I finally got the thing started up.

I figured I'd better get the hang of how to operate the machine before I hooked my valuable body up to it, so I started twisting various dials and flipping switches to see what they would do. To my surprise, as I twisted the dials, things around me started changing. One dial, turned to the left, made the room very cold. The reason for this was apparent when I looked out the window and saw all the ice covering our planet. I turned it back to where I thought it had been before and mushroom clouds started sprouting everywhere. I was glad I had decided to practice for awhile first. One dial, when turned slightly to the right, fixed it so JFK hadn't been killed, and now all the instructions for the machine and the posters on the wall were in German. Well, he told us he was a Berliner. We just didn't listen. I turned that dial back in a hurry.

It took awhile, but I finally got everything back to pretty much where it had been when I started. I was relieved. So was the dinosaur in the window.

At this point I figured I knew about as much about the machine as I ever would, unless I read the instructions, and that's not going to happen, so I hooked my body up to the machine with every loose wire I could find and turned it on full blast. Nothing happened. I began turning each of the dials, first one way, then the other. Then I yanked on all the levers, pressed all the buttons, and opened and closed all the little drawers. Still nothing. The world around me was changing all over the place, but I wasn't getting any reaction from my body at all.

I cranked up the power, diverting massive amounts of electricity from the rest of the facility so I could really give my body a blast. I really socked it to myself, as the kids say. Still nothing.

People who have heard me tell this story down at the coffee shop have speculated that the machine couldn't fix it so I had never been killed, because it had already fixed it so I had never been born. In order to fix it so I hadn't been killed, they told me, I should have reversed the not-being-born part first. When I asked them where they got all this information about a machine they'd never seen, and didn't really know existed— they only had my word for it, after all. And I lie all the time—they said sometimes they just knew things, that's all. So I guess that's what happened. Anyway, whatever the reason was, the damn thing didn't work.

Finally, when the machine started shorting out, and smoke started rolling out of my body in places where there should be no smoke, I realized it was no use. I'd given my body everything the machine had. And it wasn't enough. Sadly, I pulled the plug on myself. I would have wanted it that way, I figured.

I unhooked my body and started dragging it back home. I was tempted to just leave it where it was. The hell with it. I was tired of lugging it around. Let the cleaning people deal with it. That's what they're paid for. But I decided that wouldn't be respectful. I'd been through a lot with this body. I should take it home with me and put it in a place of honor. Then when I got tired of it I could dump it somewhere out back. A place of honor out there. I owed it that much.

I started dragging it back out of the facility, muttering about the whole thing being bullshit, which it was, and vowing to get revenge on somebody for this, which I never did. Getting out of the building was easier than getting in, because all the guards were pointing the other way. So I didn't really need to hit them with fire extinguishers. But I did anyway. I guess I was just in a bad mood.

I made my way out past the sleeping guard. As an afterthought I went back in and stole some stuff. Might as well. Everybody else was doing it. I put the stolen stuff in my body's pockets and under its shirt until it looked like a covered wagon. At least I had finally found a use for it. At least it was good for something.

Just as I got my body back out onto the street, clouds began forming over my head, thunderstorms began racing in from all directions, and lightning bolts began furiously blasting my corpse. Apparently, assert my friends at the coffee shop, who seem to know everything about meteorology as well, my body had been zapped with so much electricity, it had become the greatest lightning conductor of all time. It was being hit by every lightning bolt west of the

Rockies. My body was being blasted all up and down the street.

And the lightning wasn't all. I could have gotten used to that. But the furious winds that accompanied the thunderstorms were picking up all the loose debris in the area, including me, and hitting my body in the face with it. And my ghostly body kept being picked up and blown half a mile away and having to walk back. So, like I said, it wasn't just the lightning that was the problem.

When the storms finally started to subside, and I was just starting to think the worst was over, I felt myself being sucked towards my body by some powerful unseen force. I didn't have time to think of what to do. There was no time to think. There was only time to act. I turned to run away, but the irresistible force was pulling me in. I realize now that I wasn't thinking clearly at this point. I shouldn't have been resisting. I should have been running delightedly towards my body, not away from it. But in the end it didn't matter which way I tried to run. The force was too strong.

Suddenly, with an unpleasant "thuck", I was sucked back into my body. And if you're looking for an uncomfortable experience, I'd recommend that. It's kind of like being sucked headfirst into an ATM machine, if you've ever done that. Anyway, that's what I'd compare it to. That's what it reminded me of.

Once I was inside my body again I tried to look around, but everything was black. I wriggled around a little bit until I had repositioned myself enough so I could see out the eyes. Then I wriggled a little more until I heard a small click. That did it. My spirit and body were one again. I was alive! I wriggled some more to see if I could get back out, but I couldn't.

I sat up and checked to make sure I was all there. I wasn't. Two of my toes had been blasted off, and a small unimportant part of my skull was gone. I saw a squirrel running off with that. Plus, it looked like some asshole had filled my shirt with liquor bottles. But I figured it was close enough. I was mostly back the way I used to be. While I was checking myself out for any other damage, and looking for a kneecap that had rolled away somewhere, a car ran over me.

After a few more lightning strikes, I came back to life again. I got out of the street quicker this time.

CHAPTER SIXTEEN

"**F**rank Burly is back from the dead and raring to go!" That's what my advertisement in the next day's paper said.

That enthusiastic headline was a bit of an exaggeration, to be honest. I wasn't completely back. I was still 20% dead. But I figured that was close enough. My left nostril and right eyelid didn't work. Which meant I didn't take a good flattering picture anymore. So I mostly handed out old pictures. People looked at them and asked who it was a picture of. I usually told them to just take the picture. It's a free picture, isn't it? Just take it. What do you care who it's a picture of?

My upper lip was on the fritz too. It drooped down over my mouth and flapped disconcertingly when I talked, often standing straight out towards the client when I was alarmed. Sometimes I had to lower my rates a little to get clients to put up with this. Sometimes I just had to give them a pocket calendar.

I knew I wouldn't win any beauty contests looking like this, but I had never won any before either. I guess I should stop entering them. I should start being more realistic. But I didn't see why my looks should affect my detective business. I don't solve cases with my face. So I didn't worry about it.

I tried to get my landlord to lower my rent since I was 20% dead and presumably wouldn't be using all of the office anymore, but he said the remaining 80% of me should drop dead too. Everybody's a wise guy. Everybody has a sense of humor.

You're probably wondering how I could even be a detective again—I still hadn't been born, I still didn't have a valid PI license, I wasn't bonded, I didn't have any of the documentation you need to operate a detective agency—but after all I'd been through I just figured the hell with the paperwork. If City Hall or the Logic Police wanted to kick up a big stink about it, they knew where to find me, presumably. Meanwhile, I had to make a living.

To my surprise, I didn't get any flak from the authorities at all. It turned out City Hall had bigger things to worry about than technically nonexistent detectives like myself. The mass hallucinations that had been plaguing the city for months had stopped coming and going. Now they came and stayed.

Among other things, Central City now seemed to be ruled by a small army detachment from Peru, under a Captain Hernandez. Citizens were being ordered to "Bow Faces In Mud" when the Captain came by. If that wasn't possible because of the lack of mud, they would be ordered to "Make Mud". Plus, all of our lakes and mountains—remember them?—were gone. And there was only half a sun in the sky. These changes did not make the voters happy. Quite the reverse. And there was an election coming. So City Hall was frantic.

And the problems weren't just confined to Central City. The whole country was a mess. The federal government, which had spent the entire year doing nothing but brilliant things suddenly couldn't do anything right. The dollar collapsed overnight. So did the penny. And that, I'm told, had never happened before. One of our inalienable rights disappeared, even though the Constitution said that was impossible. And the day after I came back from the dead, somebody noticed that one of the Dakotas was gone. The best one, too.

Government spokesmen were spinning these events for all they were worth, making it sound like the President meant for that to happen, and it was good, it was part of his Bold Plan For A New America #6, but nobody was buying it. As a result, the incumbent party was looking pretty bad heading into the election season. And I was glad. I had lost confidence in the current administration. They shouldn't have erased me from existence like that. And the meat they shoved through my bars shouldn't have been lamb. When you do things like that to me, you lose my vote.

It was while I was reading in the paper about the latest government blunder—something about trading landmarks for hostages—that Ed and Fred arrived in my office demanding to know how I did it. They wanted to do it too, whatever it was.

"How did I do what?"

"You're alive," said Ed. "You're not a ghost anymore. Tell us how you did it."

"And what on Earth happened to your upper lip?" asked Fred.

"I don't have to tell you anything," I said, self-consciously covering up my droopy lip with my hand. "Piss off."

"What!"

"You heard."

I hadn't forgotten all the trouble they had caused me in the past. I don't forget things like that right away. You have to wait awhile. A few weeks, anyway. I didn't feel I owed them anything. I got up and opened the door, repeating my request that they piss off, and indicating that this was a door they could conveniently piss off through.

"You'd better tell us," said Ed, dangerously.

"If you don't, there could be trouble," added Fred.

I opened the door a little wider.

"Piss off," I reminded them.

They left, vowing revenge, which, as you know, is how I usually leave places. But I almost never come back. I'm usually bluffing. They weren't bluffing. They did come back.

A few hours later, I heard distant screaming in the streets, and the soft pattering of people fainting onto concrete. I looked out the window. Thousands of ghosts were coming up the street towards my building. Many of them were wearing ghostly army helmets. And they had gotten a ghost cannon from someplace.

I locked the door to my office and put a small chair under the knob.

The ghost army stopped in front of my building and began firing cannon shells into it. The shells passed harmlessly through the building—they were as insubstantial as the ghosts—but they were loud, and they were scaring the hell out of everybody. Once the ghosts felt that their target had been properly softened up, they charged into the building with an unearthly yell, and started up the stairs towards my office.

I went to the back window, with the idea of going down the fire escape, and never coming back, maybe making a new life for myself in a different building, but there were already ghosts climbing up the fire escape towards me. So that was out.

I thought for a moment, then put an additional chair against the door, and one on the fire escape.

The ghost army reached my office door and rattled the knob. It was locked. They paused and then rattled it again. Still locked. They discussed this development with each other in low tones—I distinctly heard the words "It's locked, I tell you" and "try it again, Sergeant"—then, after some more knob rattling and another pause, they started oozing through the walls into my office.

It was an uncomfortable position for me to be in. As insubstantial as ghosts are, they can still pack a wallop. They had killed me before. They could do it again. Even easier this time, because there were more of them. And they had artillery. I couldn't give them what they wanted—tell them how to get back into their bodies the way I had. I didn't even know how I did it. I think I just got lucky. Plus, they didn't seem to have any bodies to get back into. I wasn't sure what the rules were, but I was pretty sure you needed a body for something like this.

As I backed up away from the ghosts, who were yanking at the cannon, trying to get it through the wall, my glance happened to fall on a newspaper on my desk that was covered with headlines about how incompetent the government was. That should have given me an idea, but it didn't. Which was too bad, because I needed an idea right now. I looked around in the drawers of my desk. No ideas in there. I asked the nearest ghost if he had any ideas. He didn't. He didn't even know he was supposed to be thinking of any.

Finally I decided to just fall back onto my old standby plan—the plan that I always use when I don't have any ideas. Stall. Play for time and running room. I would promise to give them what they wanted. I knew I wouldn't be able to deliver on that promise, but that would be a long time from now. Time I could spend being alive.

I stopped backing up, faced the army, and held up a restraining hand. They stopped and looked at me suspiciously. A few fired shots at my hand. I put it in my pocket. The firing stopped. A few of the ghosts watched my pocket in case that hand came out again, while the rest lowered their weapons and listened to what I had to say.

I told the ghosts that I was touched by their

plight and promised that I would show them how they could become real men again just like me.

"Will our lips droop like that?" asked one of the ghosts.

I decided I shouldn't try to make the deal sound too good. Otherwise they might smell a rat. "More," I said.

CHAPTER SEVENTEEN

Though it had been privy to some unusual sights over the past few months, Central City had never seen a ghost army parading down the street led by a half-dead detective with a droopy eye and a floppy lip. So we were something new. A crowd gathered to watch us. A few took shots at us, and our boys let loose a couple of deafening cannon blasts in return, but neither side could actually hurt the other. So the firing quickly ceased and we continued our march in peace.

When we got to the government facility we found we were strangely unopposed. No one tried to stop us. No one checked our ID to make sure we were the right army or anything. There were no sentries in sight. I took us around to where the sleeping guard had been, so I could show everybody my trick for getting in, but he was gone too. That kind of pissed me off. When you don't know much, you like to show off the few things you do know.

"This was the only way to get in before," I told the ghosts. "Through here."

"Let's go in the main gate," said Fred.

"All right, but this side gate used to be important. Remember that."

"Yeah, yeah, let's go."

We went around to the front.

I marched the army into the facility's main building, then down the empty corridors, pointing out where each guard used to be, and how hard it used to be to get past this point here, and how mean the guard was down that hallway, and so on, to the uninterested ghosts, until we got to the room the Clarence machine was in.

I tried the door, but it was locked. The army tried a few cannon blasts, but the shells just went right through the door and out of the building. We had no idea where the shots ended up, but after we had fired four or five of them a phone next to us started ringing. We didn't answer it.

I told the ghosts I thought I knew where the key to the door was. They said I'd better. I laughed and said "good joke", then started leading them to Albert Conklin's office.

The door to Conklin's office was open, so we trooped in without knocking. Conklin was surprised to see us, but not very.

"Figures," he said, and resumed cleaning out his desk and putting everything into boxes.

I asked what was going on. Why was the building so empty? Even my guard was gone. He stopped packing and looked at me for a moment, as if trying to decide whether to bother to answer me or not, while the ghosts waited patiently, with only a few occasionally saying "boo" and the others saying "quiet".

"We're being shut down," he said finally. "We couldn't provide our service anymore so they're closing the facility."

"What service? What the heck do you do here, anyway? What's it all about?"

"Well, as you might have guessed, the Clarence machine wasn't designed just to make it so you were never born. The government doesn't spend that kind of time and money on anything so trivial as...well...you."

"I guessed that," I lied.

"Its primary purpose was to undo governmental mistakes before any nosey voters found out about them."

I said I had guessed that too. Everyone in the room suggested I be quiet for awhile and let the man talk, before something bad happened to me. That sounded like good advice, so I became quiet.

"You've got the floor, Conklin," I said.

"The machine was completed eight months ago," Conklin said. "To test it, we corrected a few governmental mistakes from the past. We got Pancho Villa off of the Supreme Court, and detonated the first hydrogen bomb at Bikini Atoll in the South Pacific, instead of Carnegie Hall in New York. The machine worked perfectly. Those original blunders just faded away, like they never happened. Old timers who could have sworn they saw Jascha Heifetz and his violin blown through the side of the Chrysler Building just think they saw a hallucination now. Then, just for the hell of it, we sank the Bismarck. And lucky for Johnny Horton we did. His 'Let's All Take A Ride On The Bismarck' had been a flop."

"I've never heard that song now," I said.

"Quiet," said everybody.

"We quickly realized that we had a powerful tool in our hands. We could call anything in history a mistake, and then just fix it. We could make our political party the only party that ever existed, because it was a mistake that there were others, or make any one of us here in the department the hereditary King Of The United States, because it was a mistake that we were clerks."

He opened one of the boxes he had packed and looked wistfully at a crown. Then he put it back and closed up the box. "But we soon learned we shouldn't meddle in the past, not even for a good cause. History is complicated, and altering any part of it can cause unforeseen problems. The Lusitania can't sink if you've just fixed it so it was never built. And if it didn't sink you've got a whole shipload of people—who should be lying safely on the bottom of the ocean—wandering around the planet for fifty or sixty years altering world events in ways you can't imagine, much less control. And then they have kids they shouldn't have had, who alter even more events. And the kids have cats you don't know about. And so on. It's a mess, believe me."

"Why would the government care about problems caused in the past?" I asked. "No skin off their nose. They live here in the good old present with us."

No one told me to be quiet. Everyone seemed to feel that was a pretty good question.

Conklin sighed. "Because by altering the past we ended up affecting the present. Members of our research team suddenly started disappearing. We didn't know why at first. We didn't connect it with anything we had done. But then we discovered that one of our men disappeared because his grandfather had been killed in a bar fight with the crew of the battleship Maine in 1911. He had said their battleship was crap, and they had said it wasn't. A fight followed, resulting in his death. That bar fight should never have happened. The Maine should have gone down in 1898. But because of our meddling, it hadn't. After several more of our people disappeared, including the head of the department, word came down from the new head of the department that all meddling with the past had to stop. It was putting all of us in danger."

I noticed a sign on the wall put out by the Government Printing Office that had a drawing of a monkey writing in a history book, with the slogan: "Only A Monkey Monkeys With The Past."

"Is that why that sign is up there?"

"Yes. That should have been an end to it, but a little while later, at an office party, one of the funnier bureaucrats in our department, who had a lampshade on his head at the time if I remember correctly, suggested having Amelia Earhart make a surprise attack on Japan in 1937. She was heading that way anyway on her round the world flight. Why not divert her? Maybe take out the Japanese leadership before the war even started. The Japanese aren't the only people who can make sneak attacks, he reminded us. Us Yanks can do it too. Well, I guess everybody had had a little too much to drink. We decided to do it."

"You'd forgotten what the monkey said," I said, pointing at the sign.

"Yes, well, we'd been drinking, as I said. Anyway, she never completed her mission. We know now that she was shot down and crashed on the lawn of the Imperial Palace in Tokyo, and died crawling towards the Emperor with a knife in her teeth. There was a big diplomatic uproar about the whole thing. It made the Japanese so mad they attacked Pearl Harbor, of all places.

"We tried to undo what we'd done, but only succeeded in blowing up the Hindenburg and making Lou Gehrig sick. On top of that, three more of our technicians vanished without a trace, and I've got a Hitler mustache now."

"I'd shave that off if I were you," I recommended.

"I do shave it off, but it keeps growing back."

I thought about this. "Try shaving it off. See if that helps."

Conklin ignored this advice. "At the time, we didn't know where Earhart's body had ended up. We assumed it would never be found. She was lost in 1937, and presumably they'd been looking for her ever since. If they hadn't found the body by now they probably never would. Then one of our guys yelled 'Hey! Some guy just found Earhart! And he's on TV! Shit!'

"Everyone crowded around the TV saying 'shit'. Then the big boss came in and saw what was going on. After awhile he left without saying anything except 'shit'.

"We knew it would only be a matter of time before everything came out in the open, including the existence of the Clarence machine."

"So what?" I asked. "That's not such a big scandal. The government has weathered bigger scandals than that before." I tried to think of an example, but all I could think of were airports.

"Like airports," I said.

He looked at me like I was stupid. Okay, maybe I am stupid, but I don't like people looking at me that way. I started to ball up my fist.

"If everything came out," he explained, "voters would realize that their representatives weren't brilliant men, but in fact were idiots with a machine that could fix their mistakes for them. We couldn't let that happen. We liked it that people thought we were smart. So we solved the problem by simply removing you from the equation. If you didn't exist, you could never find Earhart's body, and everyone would be in the clear."

"Slick," I said, impressed. "That could work."

"It did work," he reminded me. "And since then we've been very careful to only use the machine for the purpose it was originally designed. We've left the past completely alone and concentrated on fixing current governmental mistakes—everything from major problems, like global flattening, to minor embarrassments, like some county dog catcher catching the wrong dog. In every case the machine has worked perfectly.

Each mistake has been erased, and the voters have never known anything about them."

"So... everything's all right then?" I asked. I was getting a little lost.

"No. A couple of weeks ago, we came in to work and found that the Clarence machine had been broken. It looked like someone had been messing around with it, kicking it and spilling mustard on it. They had even taken some of the pieces off and lost them, then tried to replace them with pieces from a typewriter and that old refrigerator over there."

Everyone looked at me.

"Hi, everybody," I said.

"Since the machine was broken," Conklin went on, "the problems the politicians brought in to us that day couldn't be fixed. And the public, which was used to seeing brief hallucinations by now—and in fact had started to like them, to view them as a new kind of cheap entertainment—was suddenly confronted with hallucinations that didn't go away: real nuclear explosions, genuine collisions with other planets, and all-conquering foreign armies that took our land and didn't give it back three seconds later. These sorts of things did not sit well with the public. Everyone began demanding explanations. Newspapers called for investigations. All hell was breaking loose.

"The government, of course, was frantic. They demanded the Clarence machine be put back into operation this instant—it was the first time I had ever seen the federal government actually stamp its feet—but they were told it wasn't possible. The machine needed a complete overhaul, and wouldn't be operational again for months."

I didn't see what the big problem was with all this. "So what's a few months more or less?" I asked. "Whenever the machine is fixed, you can just change all this back. It'll be like it never happened."

"We don't have a few months. The administration is really going to take it on the chin in the coming elections, if the polls are right. The public views us as incompetents who can't do anything right. The Clarence machine won't be on line again until after the election. So the administration will be swept out of office and our opponents will have the machine."

"Oops."

"Yes. That's why they've ordered the machine to be dismantled, the blueprints shredded, and everyone in the facility reassigned. They don't want their political opponents to be able to use any of this stuff. And that's why the facility was nearly empty when you arrived with your friends."

Everyone in the room was quiet for a moment.

"I told you I'd find out in the end," I said.

"Yes, you did. I remember."

"Score one for me."

He nodded and made a small mark on a piece of paper.

The ghosts had been listening to all this very politely, showing remarkable patience. Finally one of them cleared his throat pointedly.

"Oh yeah," I said, "there's another problem. There are all these ghosts here."

"Yes, I'm sorry about that," said Conklin.

"You're sorry? You mean it's your fault?" asked Ed.

Conklin sighed and nodded. "I'm afraid it is. Each mistake the government made got people killed who shouldn't have died yet. And when we fixed the mistakes, we tended to kill even more. That's bureaucracy for you. Hence all the ghosts, I'm told."

"Fix it back," said Fred, quietly.

"Can't," shrugged Conklin. "As I said, the machine is broken, and it's being dismantled as we speak."

The ghosts were crestfallen. They stood there sadly for a moment, then started loading up their cannon and swiveling it around so it would be pointing at both Conklin and myself.

That gave me an idea. "Follow me everybody."

I edged past the ghosts out into the corridor. Conklin followed, wondering. Then the ghosts looked at each other, shrugged, and started following me too.

Everyone wondered what my idea was. My idea was it would be harder to kill me out in the corridor. I would have more running room out there.

As soon as I got outside the door, I started running like hell, but my feet slipped on the highly polished floor. I landed on my face and, legs still churning, skidded into a room full of experimental machines.

Everyone followed me into the room and looked around at all the gadgets.

"This is your idea?" asked Fred, dubiously.

"Uh...yeah," I said, legs still churning.

There was a long pause.

"Explain your idea to us," said Ed.

"When?"

"Now."

"Er..." I looked around the room for an idea. Suddenly, to my surprise, I got one. "Hey, yeah!" I said to myself. "That could work. And even if it didn't, at least it would buy me some time, and I could make a run for it later." At this point I realized I had been talking to myself out loud all this time—really loud. Some of the ghosts had their hands over their ears. I stopped talking. I'd already said too much.

"What could work?" asked Fred.

I explained my idea to the ghosts.

It had suddenly occurred to me that if ghosts couldn't be alive, the next best thing would be if they could at least operate as if they were living people. Some of these new gadgets might be able to help them do that.

The first thing they needed was substance, of course. I'd been a ghost myself, so I knew what a strong gust of wind could do.

One of the inventions stacked up in the corner of the room was a suit designed to help soldiers who had been blown to bits stay on the job and keep fighting for Freedom, or against Freedom, depending on who the President was at the time. It was an intricate exoskeleton suit that responded to the thoughts of the wearer.

I had a couple of the ghosts try on the suits.

They were dubious at first, but soon they were prancing around like real humans, making all kinds of noise with their feet and leaving footprints all over the place. Then they had an impromptu race to the end of the hall. Then they fought. All the ghosts watching this got very excited and clamored for suits of their own. Conklin, who was turning out to be not such a bad sort, handed out the suits, while I looked over the other inventions in the room.

There was a gadget that kept your face in place and kept the features on that face from drifting around. It was designed to help politicians keep a straight face when they made campaign promises. Conklin said it was intended to be a gag, but Washington had ordered 100,000 of them. A device like that would be handy for ghosts too, I thought, so I had Conklin start handing out some of those. Then I found some oversized artificial digestive tracts which had been invented so government bigwigs could eat twenty times more than a normal human. Ghosts would certainly be able to use a digestive tract, even if it was comically big. So each ghost got one of those too.

Some of the gadgets I found weren't of any use to us, like the machine that made lies be true, and the machine that would squeeze votes out of us and then blow our heads off, but they were the exceptions. Most of the stuff would come in handy in one way or another.

Since everybody else was getting something, I felt I should get something too. So I grabbed one of those machines that makes all the evil people in the world six inches tall. With a machine like that, my job would be a snap. I turned it on to test it, and Conklin and I both became really short. I turned the knob back to where it was before, then put the machine back where I found it. I decided I didn't want it anymore.

When I had successfully outfitted all the ghosts with everything they would need to rejoin the land of the living, we happily exited and let Conklin get back to his packing.

CHAPTER EIGHTEEN

I always like to end my exciting stories pretty much back where they started, so readers will get the feeling that whatever happens in this crazy world of ours, old Frank Burly will always be right back where he started. He's not going anyplace. So I guess I should stop here, and not move on to being hanged by those vigilantes out West. That belongs in another adventure.

As this story ends, everything has pretty much gotten back to normal in Central City. The hallucinations have stopped, thanks to my intervention. Now when something bad happens, it's real.

And the town's ghost problem has been solved as well. The ghosts are still there, of course, but they are all productive members of the community now. Instead of haunting houses and slouching around town making everybody nervous, they are hard at work every day serving up hamburgers at fast food joints, guarding warehouses at night, filling up gumball machines, and doing other low profile, but necessary, productive, and satisfying jobs. Thanks to their special survival gear, they can stay substantial for a full eight hour shift. And after working all day, they're too tired to do any haunting, even if they wanted to. Just eat some dinner, watch some ghost stories on TV, then hit the sack.

That's not to say that the ghosts are actually good at these jobs they're doing. Even with their special equipment they're still slow and clumsy and tend to drop things a lot. So if you've noticed that the service you're getting these days isn't as good as it used to be, or the products you buy look like they were put together by someone wearing a catcher's mitt, or the people who are supposed to be helping you suddenly just disappear and never come back, now you know why.

The whole Clarence machine thing eventually came out in the papers. You can't stop people from finding out about things. At least not since I wrecked that machine.

When the story first broke, a lot of people were angry. There were calls for investigations, demands for resignations, and so on. All the usual stuff. But pretty soon the public's tone changed to one of admiration. Pretty slick cover-up work, a lot of people thought. That's the kind of people we want representing us. Sneaky little shits like that. Why didn't they tell us they were sneaky little shits instead of pretending to be self-promoting idiots?

Now the word is that the old sneaky regime might be swept back into power in the next election, despite its obvious flaws. The public wants to get some of that shitty sneakiness working for them.

So things worked out pretty well for just about everybody. I'm still not born, and I'm still regularly struck by lightning, and women I ask out say I smell dead to them, but you can't have everything.

I saw Ed and Fred one last time. They had really landed on their feet. Instead of working at some crappy low-wage job like the other ghosts, they had opened up a detective agency on the floor below mine, and were cleaning up on cases where the client didn't want to ride the elevator up the last eight feet just to get to me. I congratulated them on their success, and they said they owed it all to me. And I said I guessed that was about right.

As a parting gesture, they told me who the real murderer was in that case I told you about earlier—the one where I rented the stadium. In fact, they brought him into my office, looking a little shamefaced. He was a ghost now too. Ironically, I had gotten him killed when I was messing around with the Clarence machine. Thanks to me, he had gotten beaten to death by Jack Dempsey in a title fight he knew nothing about. There's some justice there somewhere, I suppose.

When he admitted his guilt to me, I couldn't believe it.

"But you had an ironclad alibi!" I said.

"Maybe so, but I still did it."

"Well, I'll be a son of a gun! Did you really

shoot all those men on that troopship I was guarding?"

"I sure did!"

And we all had to laugh.

When Ed and Fred left, I waved goodbye to them, and I even blew them a little kiss. It was nice of the boys to solve my murder for me, but I still think they're a couple of pricks.